Dustman to Ashes

By Rosemonde S. Peltz

DUSTMAN TO ASHES

Dustman to Ashes

ROSEMONDE S. PELTZ

PUBLISHED FOR THE CRIME CLUB BY
DOUBLEDAY & COMPANY, INC.
GARDEN CITY, NEW YORK
1987

Library of Congress Cataloging-in-Publication Data

Peltz, Rosemonde S.
Dustman to ashes.

I. Title.
PS3566.E44D8   1987   813'.54   86-29220
ISBN 0-385-23552-6

For two fine people,
Jean Rose
and
Harrilyn Parsons,
with great affection for each

Dustman to Ashes

RUMSDEN VALLEY CONSTABULARY
THE COTSWOLDS
WINTER 1975

"Yes, sir."

Caywood squatted close to the body, avoiding as much of the congealed blood as possible. What he saw was a middle-aged man of medium height and medium build, brown hair, brown eyes, who appeared to have had his head bashed in by the proverbial blunt instrument. He looked up from the body, glancing around the yard, sizing up the geography again. To his left was the church of St. Mary's, and beyond it was what he assumed to be the vicarage joined to the church by an umbilical cord of a sheltered stone walk. Directly ahead of him was a small honey stone building. Caywood pointed to it.

"Church hall," Kirk responded.

"And beyond it?"

"Woods, thick and dense. We've circled through. Found nothing."

Caywood turned his attention to the body once more. "Doesn't look like he was dressed for the weather."

"It was relatively warm yesterday, Inspector. Didn't start snowing until this morning."

"Looks like someone got him yesterday, late evening," Caywood said.

"Yes, sir. He's going to freeze if Dr. Wick doesn't come soon."

The body was clothed in a dark green work uniform, the cheap variety available in any number of stores. Caywood pushed the victim's collar wider apart. There was no chain, the wrists were bare.

"Not even a wristwatch. No ring," Caywood said.

"Vicar said he wasn't married."

"Wedding bands do not a marriage make, eh, Sergeant?"

"Tell me about it," Kirk muttered in disgust.

"Trouble with Angela?" Caywood asked.

"She's leaving me."

"I'm sorry to hear that, Harry. I hope you can put it right." Caywood stood up, straightening his back that creaked in protest. "Lord, I'm getting old for this kind of business. Get to a phone and light a match under our police surgeon, please, Harry. There's a good fellow. Tell him we're freezing as stiff as the corpse that's awaiting him."

Caywood shielded himself against the wind and lit a cigarette while he waited for Kirk to return. He pulled the flaps out of his brown tweed cap to cover his ears, now cold enough to break off, and turned his back to the shifting wind once more. His head struck the yellow tarpaulin and snow flew off in all directions. Hastily he stooped down again and systematically began fishing in the victim's pockets. Kirk returned to watch him deftly examine the body without moving it a single millimeter. He poked two long fingers in an old-fashioned watch pocket and retrieved an ornate gold pocket piece. He held it out, dangling, floating from its heavy antique chain.

"Fancy," Caywood appraised it. "Apparently robbery wasn't the motive, or else our murderer didn't know about watch pockets, in which case robbery was still the motive."

"Never rob a poor man," Kirk said as he walked up.

"A maxim for all crooks to live by," Caywood agreed.

Caywood held the watch by the end of its chain and let it rock in the wind. Kirk handed him a heavy plastic bag. The case was engraved in an intricate design that seemed familiar. Caywood deposited the watch in the evidence bag and handed it to Kirk. Then he knelt down again, folding his long legs under him, and peered at the body one last time.

Tall, spartan, lean Harry Kirk, as hard as any stone in St. Mary's Church, stood behind him and shielded his inspector from the wind. While he waited, Kirk reached up and secured the old yellow canvas tarp on its rods as tightly as possible. Accumulating snow was now freezing and threatening to collapse onto the body. Caywood stood up slowly, waiting for his knees to creak, and smiled gratefully when they didn't.

Kirk noticed. "Something funny?" he asked.

"No, Harry. Private joke."

Kirk smiled, not knowing why, except he liked his chief inspector most of the time and he'd learned to humor him. He laughed at the inspector's jokes and smiled when Caywood smiled.

"Get one of the constables over here to wait for Dr. Wick. I'm going into the church."

St. Mary's Church was the focal point of Cheamley. It rose above all the cottages and spread to one side to encompass the church hall and to the other to the rectory. At its rear were the woods of Mayfest.

The high gate was in good repair, with snow now spread like a mantle over the gabled roof. Caywood retreated to it and stood protected while he waited for Kirk. The door to the church was framed by six receding semicircular arches, each emboldened by carvings of fierce monsters and devils that age had worn to present meekness. He could no longer tolerate the cold and went inside.

When he got past the great wooden doors and into the comparative warmth of the yellow-gray stone foyer of the country church, Caywood slapped his wet cap against his thigh and tried to stamp life back into his frozen legs. He waited.

Detective Chief Inspector Caywood did not fit the mold of a country policeman. Now that he was breathing on middle age, he fit it even less. His shaggy blond hair was gray at the edges, but he still had a full head of it. He combed it carefully in front of his younger, totally bald sergeant. Thin, with the bare beginning of a sagging middle, Caywood always stood particularly straight when a mirror was in the vicinity. The fine wrinkles that divided his forehead and surrounded his mouth had not been there two years before. He needed eyeglasses through which to focus tired blue eyes, but when he got some he rarely used them. Caywood enjoyed his work, and he didn't want anyone to think he might be getting too old for the job. He was in his prime, a long way to go before he was sized for a shroud.

He stood in the foyer and stamped his feet again. The clatter of his boots brought a tweedy Altar Guild lady whose job it was to guide tourists through St. Mary's. She came in that half-run, half-lope of a determined ostrich. Caywood recognized the soft, hushed, clipped speech of a church guide.

"You are in St. Mary's, sir, one of the finest examples of—"

"Yes, I know," Caywood interrupted.

"Oh . . ." her voice trailed off in disappointment.

Caywood understood the message. He walked courteously in front of the lady and deposited ten pence in the visitor's box.

"Please take a church folder."

"Thank you, Miss . . . ?"

"Mrs. Charles." She smiled.

"I'm Detective Chief Inspector Caywood, Mrs. Charles."

"Oh, I hope nothing is wrong." The ostrich transformed rapidly into a wren.

"There is a problem, quite an unpleasant one. So please stay in the church."

She stared up at Caywood's lean face.

"Someone's dead. That's it, isn't it?"

"Yes, someone's dead, so please stay in the church. Would you help me, please?"

"Oh yes, of course, Inspector."

Kirk strode in, brushing snow off his glistening head, ignoring what was melting in his beard. The two of them stood at equal height, like two waterfowl making their own pond as they dripped in place and flapped their arms to dry off.

"Mrs. Charles, this is Sergeant Kirk. Can you help us find the vicar?"

"Who is dead?" she asked, ignoring his request.

"That's one of the things we are investigating," Caywood said patiently. She reminded him of his mother in Bath. "Could you please direct us to the vicar?"

"Yes, of course," she gave in. They heard footsteps. "Oh, here he comes." She stepped back.

Caywood turned toward the reverberating sound of the vicar's steady gait. He waited, and saw the church for the first time since his brain had thawed.

There was a central aisle perpendicular to the yellow-gray stone altar that was covered by white linen. Above the altar and well beyond the organ was a great circular stained glass window that let in no light today. Although the candles that bulged in the massive silver holders were not burning, there was an aroma of perfume and tallow still in the air. Three tall windows guarded the narrow side aisles. Behind the altar was a huge organ that looked so new as to be out of place in this ancient church. Choir stalls extended on either side of the organ, while an intricately carved baptismal font stood on the left. The musty air of generations past clung to the stones and hung in the air. Caywood wondered how Cheamley could support all of this.

The vicar passed in front of the altar and stopped to pick up a kneeler that had been kicked into the aisle. Caywood smiled at the housekeeping. He and Kirk stood on the same cold stones that floored the entire church. Behind and against the left side wall was a table on which were the usual contribution box, postcards, pamphlets, and Leatherette bookmarks. A vase of wilting flowers beginning to reek of rot was surrounded by withered petals.

"I'm Edmund Morgan," the vicar said, extending a strong right hand.

"Chief Detective Inspector Caywood, and this is Sergeant Kirk."

Morgan turned to Mrs. Charles. "I wonder if you might help Mrs. Harper pack the old hymnals in the storage room?"

"Yes, of course, Vicar." Her face said she'd like to stay and hear what was happening.

Edmund Morgan had straight black hair that was turning gray about his ears and neck. It fell evenly all around as if suspended from the bald spot that was in the center of his head. His sharp nose supported his spectacles and hung over a salt-and-pepper mustache that spread across his upper lip. The man was short, round and wrinkled. The dark blue suit he wore was wrinkled, and his boots were muddy.

"You've seen the body and recognised the victim?" Caywood asked.

"Yes. It's our dustman, Stanley. Grisly sight. Here one day, gone the next," he said, shaking his head from side to side. He started walking toward the altar and signaled the policemen to follow. "We'll be more comfortable in the vicarage. We can sit down and have something hot to drink."

Caywood read the welcome relief on Kirk's face. "That would make me feel much better," he confessed.

They followed Morgan past the altar and out a side door to a covered walk that extended along the church to the rectory. The trees beside the walk were black skeletons dotted with snow. Caywood thought the place would be lovely in spring, but now there wasn't even the promise of anything beautiful.

The rectory was no more than a cottage, the church's poor relative. When they reached it, a middle-aged woman, brown-haired and with smooth fair skin, opened the door and waited as the three men walked toward her. "I'm glad you're back, Vicar. Suppose that murderer is still in Cheamley. It's awful, just awful."

"Inspector Caywood, this is Mrs. Shaw, who looks after me and the rectory." The woman nodded. It was then that Caywood noticed Morgan wore no wedding band.

"Yes, I know, Mrs. Shaw. It's awful. And this is Sergeant Kirk." She looked at them and again nodded ever so slightly.

"They are here to set everything straight. Now, be a good woman and pull yourself together."

"Quentin never harmed anyone, Vicar. Not ever."

"Mrs. Shaw, let's have something hot." He shook her by the shoulder and again told her to calm herself.

Then, quite suddenly, she ran away to another room. Morgan led the detectives quickly through the foyer, past the lounge, and into his study, where two small logs crackled in the fireplace.

"Please sit down, gentlemen," he invited.

Caywood unbuttoned his jacket and loosened his muffler.

"Tell me about Quentin Stanley, please." Caywood pushed himself into a comfortable position on the green leather sofa opposite the brown chair where Kirk sat.

Vicar Morgan poked the fire in an effort to extract more warmth from it and then stood before it. Caywood thought the vicar was stalling, postponing any serious conversation. Mrs. Shaw entered, still weeping a bit as she placed a heavy silver tray on the table in front of Caywood.

"I'll pour, Mrs. Shaw," the vicar said, excusing the poor woman.

The teapot sent steam upward in the study that was chilly in spite of the fire. Dampness and the musty odor of old books permeated the room. Caywood glanced around at the shelves that lined two walls. Theology, history, and fine art volumes dominated.

"Cream? Lemon?" Morgan asked.

"Neither," Caywood said and accepted a cup just as it was poured. Kirk indicated he'd like cream.

"You were asking about Quentin, Inspector," Morgan said. "He was a dustman and handyman, went house to house doing cleaning chores and odd jobs. He worked here one day during the week, another day at houses, and so on."

Mrs. Shaw came in again with a plate of dry-looking cake. "I forgot the cake," she said solemnly.

"Mrs. Shaw, how well did you know Quentin Stanley?" Caywood asked.

"All my life. He lived in Cheamley all his life, just like me," she said and began to sniffle.

"Was he married?"

"No, he never was to my knowledge."

"Thank you, Mrs. Shaw," Caywood said and indicated to the vicar that he'd finished talking to the lady for the time being.

Morgan poured another cup for the men, and Caywood took the opportunity to stand up. He did so quickly, pushing his cap into his pocket as he reached for the cup Morgan handed him. He moved closer to the fire.

"Do you know how old he was?" Caywood asked.

"No, not really," Morgan said, "but I think about my age, fifty and then some."

Caywood thought that the vicar looked considerably younger.

"He was in Cheamley when I came here," the vicar went on. "And I don't think he ever married or had any kin, actually."

"Can you think of any reason why someone should want to murder him?"

"No. I wouldn't think he was capable of causing anyone a problem; therefore, why should anyone want to kill him?"

"Still waters, Vicar. This village may seem like a quiet stream, but one never knows. How many people live in Cheamley?"

"Less than a hundred, closer to fifty. We do have people who go back and forth to other villages close by and even as far as Rumsden."

"Do you have a map of Cheamley or some plan of where your

congregation lives?" Caywood noticed that Kirk took a slab of jelly cake. "I came in the village by way of the north bridge."

"There's really very little in the way of a map. None's really needed. We're so small. I'll try to find one for you, but I've been here for years and know every soul and cobble there is."

"You said children found the body?" Caywood took another swallow of tea.

"Yes. I felt very badly about them seeing such a grisly sight."

Crumbs fell into Kirk's beard as he worked on the cake.

"I took them home just before you arrived, Inspector," Morgan said and poured a choking Kirk another cup.

"Derek and Rose Adams are the children who found the body. Apparently they were playing in the woods and started home through the cemetery when the snow got heavy."

"One wonders about children," Caywood said almost to himself and moved his wet feet closer to the dying fire. "When I drove in from the north bridge there was a newsagent on the left and there were some stone cottages in a line more or less until I arrived at St. Mary's."

"Yes," Morgan said. "The bus stops at the kiosk. The cottages are here, and beyond the woods is Mayfest."

"And there are shops across the road from the cottages, and then there is a road west of the shops, more houses, and then the river," Caywood said.

"Yes, we are divided geographically into haves and have-nots," Morgan said.

"The working class in the stone cottages, the merchants in the middle, and the wealthy beyond, by the river. Is that what you are saying?" Caywood asked.

"More or less." Morgan smiled. "The first cottage is vacant; the next houses an elderly woman named Charlotte Gill. She's quite a recluse, and next to her is Hazel Weller. Hazel, for all practical purposes, is an invalid, confined to a wheelchair. Next to her is Quentin's cottage. The cottages are identical."

"Yes," Caywood said, "one blur of yellow gray as I drove by." He was making a sketch and list as the vicar spoke.

"There's a garden between two groups of cottages, although you wouldn't know it now what with all the snow. Then there are four more cottages joined together. The Thompsons and their two children live in the first one. Mr. and Mrs. Riley are in the second. A Miss Amanda Fields lives in the third. I don't know her or Mr. Keith, who is in the last cottage. They don't attend church."

Morgan pointed out the window. "Next to us is the church hall, and as you know the cemetery extends from the church back to the woods."

Kirk sat munching on yesterday's cake, and Caywood saw him turning slightly green. The cake was obviously getting larger and larger in his mouth.

"Excuse me, Vicar. My sergeant needs to use your bathroom but is too polite to ask."

"Oh of course. Sergeant, come with me. Help yourself to cake, Inspector."

Kirk's last expression was one of eternal gratitude and warning against the cake.

Caywood smiled and poured himself another cup of tea, but set it aside until the vicar returned. He joined Morgan at the window and could feel the cold air creeping in under the sill.

"Across the road is the school, and beyond are four houses close to the river, and, of course, the pub is close to the north bridge. It's impossible to get lost." Morgan opened the tortoiseshell cigarette box that was on his desk and offered one to a grateful Caywood, who fished around for a lighter.

"Have all the inhabitants been here for a long time—that is, a long time as considered by the other villagers?"

Morgan laughed. "I'm a rank newcomer by their standards, but they ignore their vicars, as you may have suspected. I've been here about twenty years. The Sares have been here about eighteen or thereabouts, and the rest have been here since Elizabeth I rode through with her entourage. Oh, yes. Amanda Fields and Mr. Keith are truly newcomers, here only a few months."

"Vicar, where were you last night?"

"Ah, a suspect, eh?"

"No, not actually, just the plodding policeman's questions, a place for everything and so on."

"I was here, as was half the village, at various meetings and choir practice."

"We'll need a list of people here last night."

"I doubt there is one. You'll have to rely on some doddering memories and the fact that they will all vouch for their friends."

"One important thing, Vicar, we will need an investigation centre. May we impose upon you for the use of your church hall?"

"Of course. I'll handle that for you. No problem." He turned when Kirk returned to the study. "Ah, there you are, Sergeant. Another cup?"

"No, thank you, Vicar."

"Sergeant, we're to use the church hall for our centre, so we have to set that up." Caywood signaled Kirk that it was time to get on with it. "Wait for the police surgeon while I make the first foray into the victim's cottage."

Caywood and Kirk walked from the rectory, leaving the vicar to his fire, and returned to Kirk's roped-off scene of the crime. The police constable moved gingerly about the body, stamping his feet, clapping his gloved hands together in an effort to keep warm.

Caywood moved on.

If there had been something green or something flowering, the cottage would have been less forbidding. Caywood paused at the cracking door that opened directly onto a narrow footpath that paralleled the road. He turned the key the vicar had given him, pushed hard, and immediately discovered it was colder inside Quentin Stanley's cottage than it was out. Even worse, there was no electric current, so he had to grope around in the dim light until he found an oil lamp. Once lit, the flickering, smelly lamp revealed that the gray stone cottage was a hovel without any colour or any cheerful thing. The fireplace grate was empty, without evidence of a recent coal or wood fire. Caywood went from the front room to a small bedroom, a bathroom, and to the kitchen, one room smaller than another. He inspected the floors, ceilings, and walls first in each room before tackling chests, closets, and drawers.

He put the lamp on the dresser and systematically went through each drawer. Stanley's clothes were clean and patched, far beyond their prime. Next, he tore up the bed that had been poorly made at the beginning. Nothing. He found nothing in the linens, or in the mattress or under the bed. The closet held an ancient RAF great-coat hung on a peg. There were two gray caps and a dilapidated brown fedora on a shelf above the coat.

Nothing in the bathroom surprised him. Nor was the kitchen remarkable. There was a wood stove, an old-fashioned wooden box for ice, a cupboard with a mixture of cracked cups and saucers. A kettle on the stove was partially filled with ice-crusted water. Below the shelves were two drawers that Caywood took out completely and placed on the kitchen table. When he dumped the first drawer on the table the treasures of Stanley's life lay before him, several old photos and a journal; in the next drawer were coins and three five-pound notes. One of the photographs looked vaguely familiar. Then it came to him: some cinema star from the past. There were some elderly men and women in another. The last was of a child, something strange-looking about the boy.

"Find anything, Inspector?" Kirk had come in as quietly as he usually did.

"Wick finished?"

"Yes. Site's all clear now. Waiting for you."

"What did old Wick have to say about the victim?"

"Medical examiner said it was your usual blunt instrument, but that he also may have died of asphyxia."

"That's really pinning it down. What did he guess as to the time of death?"

"Did better on that, he did, Inspector. Said death occurred between 10:30 P.M. and midnight last night, Wednesday night."

"I wonder how cold it was last night. He could be off if cold froze the body or if the victim were running for his life."

"Not too cold last night, Inspector, but he's the expert; says ten-thirty to midnight."

"He can write it down and forget it until the inquest. I have to be a trifle more accurate. Please find out exactly what the weather was here last night."

"Yes, Chief Inspector."

Caywood recognised the tone of his sergeant's voice. "Quit being so agreeable." He handed Kirk the photograph of the boy.

"Look peculiar to you, Harry?"

"He's a mongoloid."

"Yes, that's it." Caywood appreciated the memory jog. "Down's syndrome is what it's called now."

"Sweet children. My older sister had one. Very sweet child."

"Do you suppose Quentin Stanley had a child? Well, no point worrying about it at this late hour. Here, take the photo, the journal, and the rest and lock them up." Caywood secured the door, and then he and Kirk walked slowly back to the graveyard. Kirk's tent still stood under the weight of the snow.

"It's too dark to do anything now," Caywood complained.

"Yes, sir."

"Good. You have your list?"

"Yes, sir. We can start in the morning."

"Well then, let's call it a night. I'll be here around eight."

"I'll have your notes typed by then if I can have them."

"Right you are." Caywood retrieved a leather book from his breast pocket and handed it to Kirk. "That's what I hoped you'd say." Then he turned and asked in an offhand manner well known to Kirk, "What do you think of this place, Harry?"

"Seems like a quiet 'mind your own business' sort of place."

"Strange place for a murder, don't you think? Peaceful place, or so they would want us to think. Good night, Harry."

"Good night, Inspector."

CHAPTER 2

Chinese Takeaway

Now the moon was coming up and the landscape was not quite so dark as Caywood drove toward Rumsden. He took greater notice of the cottages as he left. Lights were coming on, but it was still a bleak place. He felt a little warmer as soon as he'd left Cheamley.

An hour later, and with only one side trip, he had reached Bromley Square, where Eliza Crisp lived. Her car was in the park, for which he was grateful. There were times when Bromley Square and Eliza's Bentley were intimidating, but tonight was not one of them. He was too tired to care. He went through the great iron gates and avoided a few leafy branches that sprawled onto the red brick walk. There were four storeys to this impressive stone building, two flats on each floor. Through the double white door Caywood went, and through the foyer, where he ignored the lift. A clean, citrus aroma in the area was a treat to his nose. He hit the white marble steps two at a time. No matter how many times he'd trod this route, whenever his foot landed on the third step, music about marble halls started in his head, and he began to hum. He walked up a flight of steps to the next level, where Eliza's flat occupied half the floor. He had never seen the old gentleman who had the other flat and never knew who placed fresh flowers in the hallway. He rapped on the door twice before a buzzer popped the automatic lock. His boots clacked on the tinted terrazzo floor.

"You, Peter?"

"Yes. Hope you weren't expecting anyone else."

"No, but I'm not ready yet," she called from the bedroom.

"Never are," Caywood muttered as he deposited the cartons in the kitchen.

"Make some drinks or sit down or do something while I finish." He returned to the lounge and waited for her.

It was a cool, comfortable room, the walls of which were covered with pale green silk. A long emerald green sofa with black lacquer tables at either end dominated the room. The coffee table was black as well, with white and brass lamps that cast soft lights across the silver and crystal dishes sitting on it. There were one or two magazines about interiors and buildings at one end of the table, while a larger stack was on the table across the room. Chinese dogs and tigers looked down from shelves upon rows of silver boxes and art history books that lined cases at the end of the room.

Eliza entered the room. She was as tall as Peter, looked him straight in the eyes and frequently stood toe to toe. She was one of those liberated females whom Caywood thought he despised. She could direct her corporate board, run her store as tight as any admiralty ship, and still make Peter feel important. She was intelligent, attractive, and sophisticated. He never understood why she put up with him, much less loved him—or at least he thought she did.

She wore her black hair straight back in a soft bun. Her eyes were as black as her hair, her skin pale ivory. She was slim, with a good figure that she clothed as elegantly as any woman in London or Paris.

"You're awfully quiet tonight," she said as she came toward him. "Worth waiting for?"

"Aren't you a vain witch?" He kissed her. "Always worth waiting for, although there are some nights I wish I didn't have to wait as long."

She smiled. Her dress was long, black, slit up the left side to her knee. There was a collar of soft black feathers.

Caywood began to unbutton her long gloves.

"Why are you doing that? Had a devil of a time putting them on not five minutes ago."

"Do you think we're going to the Ritz?" He continued to work on her gloves.

"Why not?"

"Not on a policeman's pay."

"Well then, give it up and find a job that will pay for the Ritz. You're able."

"You're overdressed for the local café."

"I'm starving."

"Look in the kitchen. I brought Chinese."

"Damn! You didn't!" She pulled her arms away from him. "Why did you make me dress?"

"I didn't make you dress. It was your idea, my dear."

She saw the lewd smile on his face. "Never mind saying any more." Eliza pushed the black lacquered coffee table directly in front of the sofa. She caught him right on the shins. He jumped a foot.

"Easy, Eliza."

"Sit there. I'll fetch the Chinese junk." She cleared the coffee table of various cigarette boxes and crystal dishes and then threw a roll of paper towels across the table and let it run.

"Lovely lace tablecloth," he remarked, slightly fearful of the next foray.

"Wait till you see the porcelain." She returned from the kitchen in an instant and dumped three paper cartons on the table in front of him.

"Really, Eliza," he shouted.

"Really, my eye!"

"This is too much," he continued.

"You're lucky I don't put you and your Chinese takeaway straight out the door! Eat and be quiet."

"Fried rice?"

"No, thank you very much."

"Don't you think we might have plates?"

"You know where they are, Peter." She took a long gold-tipped cigarette from the box near her chair. When he returned with two of her best Turkish plates, a cloud of smoke circled her black hair. She took the plates from him back into the kitchen and handed him a blue willow number and a serving spoon and heavy silver fork.

"Oh," he said, "are we going to be that civilised? Why not eat out of the boxes with our fingers?"

"Up to you, Peter dear. Choice is yours."

He grabbed the plate from her and tossed it onto the table.

"Temper, temper, Chief Inspector," she mocked. "A policeman must be calm in every crisis."

He piled the plate with fried rice and Mongolian beef, crunching as loudly as he could on the spring onions. She ignored him and lit another cigarette. When he finished, he made coffee for them and served her a cup.

"My dinner was very good indeed," he said softly.

"Happy you enjoyed it." She put the coffee beside her on the table.

"Yes, quite good. Very new place over on Rowley Street," he said, trying to smooth over her ruffled feathers. He pulled his case from his pocket and offered her one of his cigarettes.

"No, thank you. We must clean up this mess and get rid of the filthy odor."

He heard the emphasis on "we."

"Come now, Peter, this was your idea. You don't expect me to clean up in my best dress. Just roll it up, my dear, and toss it."

"You wouldn't like me to roll up your silver and toss it, would you?"

"Up to you, Peter. After all, dinner in was your idea. Dishes are not my thing."

"Quit pouting, Eliza."

"Cut it out, Peter. You're pressing your luck. Don't expect me to clean up after you." Her voice said she meant it.

"Very well!" He picked up the cartons, plate, and whatever else got in his way and crashed it all into the dustbin. She heard the clattering breaking dish all the way in the lounge and was glad to be rid of the blue willow.

When he returned, she had everything in the room back to her satisfaction. The scene did not escape him. Caywood sat on the sofa opposite her and again offered her a cigarette. She declined.

"You really are a shrewish woman. I don't know what I do to annoy you so."

"You haven't the time for the entire list." She sipped her coffee. Caywood saw her beginning to relax.

"Why won't you marry me?" he asked softly.

"I am not going to marry you, Peter. It's bad enough for you to promise to take me out and then show up here, not only late but with paper cartons of gelatinous garbage masquerading as food. What would life be like if you had my name on the dotted line? No, thank you, Herr Inspector."

"Eliza, it's been a bloody bad day. Please don't harass me."

"I'm not harassing you. I am simply stating the fact that I am not going to take a backseat to crooks and dead people."

"I promise you. I promise you I will take you out tomorrow." Caywood hated himself for lying.

"Now we both know you are not telling the truth."

"I promise, Eliza."

The buzzer sounded.

"Who the devil is that?" Caywood demanded.

"Anthony Prentice, I hope," she answered.

"Eliza, you don't mean to tell me you're leaving me here and going out with that odd lot?"

She picked up a black velvet bag and went to the door. "Of course I am. I'd appreciate your locking up when you leave, Peter."

CHAPTER 3

Friendly Neighbors

The icy coating on the north bridge lay undisturbed until Caywood's small car crunched and slid through it. He slowed down cautiously to avoid a skid before he tucked in close to St. Mary's yard. Kirk's red beard brought him to a halt.

"Good morning, Inspector. Did you have a pleasant night?" Kirk asked as he met Caywood on the slope of Cheamley churchyard.

"Rather as cool as this place. Miss Crisp was a bit crisper than usual," Caywood replied.

"Brought Chinese, eh?" Kirk was always ahead of the game.

"You know the problem, then."

"All too well, Inspector. She doesn't like Chinese."

"No, you miss the point. I think the fact is that she would prefer it in Peking."

"Still frozen," Kirk commented.

"The ground, Miss Crisp, or both?"

"Your choice, Inspector."

Caywood got to the edge of the investigation site and began to poke and look in earnest. The rolling slopes of the churchyard merged into one another like a quiet sea. The white blanket of snow was unbroken except for the irregular gravestones that poked through. There was a hush to this end of the village, as quiet as the end of the world.

Caywood surveyed the entire area and found nothing new. "I don't find anything, Harry, but let's leave the barriers up until the snow melts and then have another go at it."

"What about the funeral?"

"What?"

"Quentin Stanley's funeral, Inspector."

"Right you are. A member of the congregation, but please check with the vicar. Maybe they can bury the poor man away from our site."

"A final resting place away from his last resting place."

Caywood raised his eyebrows at Kirk's joke as he started down the slope. "What we need to do is really get our files and incident centre set up better and with as little disruption of the church as possible. The church hall, I suspect, is the ladies' domain. We need to do it without ruffling any feathers. Ladies have a way of winning when they've a mind to. While you're at that, I'm going to start at the news kiosk and work back toward you."

Caywood pushed through the snow along the edge of the narrow village road. Sensibly he'd padded both boots the night before and worn an extra sock on his right foot. He was reasonably comfortable until two cars passed, splashing him as they moved through to larger pastures. Cheamley was as silent at the north bridge end as it had been at the cemetery. Caywood approached the newsstand.

Colourful magazines with country scenes and pretty girls on their covers lined the shelves that made the rear wall of the stone newsstand. The front wall was wooden, with a hinged upper half that swung out and up to become a roof for customers. On the shelf that extended from the lower half were two large cracked blue bowls filled with a variety of pence. Four different newspapers in separate stacks were piled between the change bowls. He wondered why the newslady had two bowls.

"Good morning."

"*Times*, please."

The lady handed him a paper as he deposited some change in the left bowl.

"Do you have any tea by some remote chance?"

"Angels will have tea soon's it's open," she told him. "Some don't like the ale." She pointed in the direction of the pub.

Caywood glanced at his watch and tightened his belt. "I'm

Detective Chief Inspector Caywood of Rumsden CID." Caywood showed his identification to the lady. "I suppose you've heard about the death of your neighbor."

"I heard it was murder, and he wasn't my neighbor."

"I thought Mr. Stanley's cottage was just over there." Caywood pointed to the cottage.

"Oh yes. I know, Inspector, but I live in Wateson," the woman said abruptly. She was neatly attired with a bright blue smock over a flowered dress. The long sleeves extended beyond the cuffs of her smock and were buttoned at the wrists. She had wavy gray hair with hints of blue that fell upon the muffler tied around her neck. She had half-frame glasses on her nose and stained gloves on her hands.

"More ink on my fingers than on the newspaper." She laughed nervously as she saw Caywood looking at her thick woolen gloves, the fingertips of which were cut out.

"Yes. Do you remember anything unusual occurring day before yesterday, Wednesday, that is?"

"No, sir."

"The usual customers came? No one you've never seen before?"

"Yes, sir. No change from the usual. No one new," she replied.

"Did you know Quentin Stanley?"

"Only when I saw him in the road. He never bought anything."

"Never a newspaper or a magazine?"

"No, Inspector. Nothing."

"Did you see him Wednesday, by any chance?"

"No, he wasn't in the road that day. Of course, I'm tending to my business, and I could have missed seeing him." Her brown eyes flashed up at Caywood.

"Right. In other words you come into Cheamley from Wateson, Mrs. . . . ?"

"Peters, Violet Peters. I drive in at six in the morning. Close at noon."

"All afternoon?"

"Oh no. I drive back to Wateson and prepare lunch for my husband. He drives back and stays open until the last bus."

"When is the last bus?"

She had a "don't you know anything?" look on her face. "Last bus arrives in Cheamley at 10:20 P.M."

"Did you like Quentin Stanley?"

"Never knew him well enough to dislike or like for that matter."

The chill in the woman's voice was as icy as the air. The only warming things in view were two porno magazines Mrs. Peters was trying to hide on the shelf behind her.

Caywood tried once more.

"Do you think any of your customers disliked Stanley?"

"That's never come up, Inspector. Never heard the man's name mentioned, matter of fact."

"Thank you, Mrs. Peters. One of my men will be back later to talk to your husband. By the way, Mrs. Peters, do you know what Quentin Stanley looked like?"

"Don't you know?" she asked in astonishment.

"Mrs. Peters, you seem to know so little about a man who lived not a hundred meters from you, I just wondered. In life, what did he look like? What did he wear usually?"

"Well, I never," she said. "He was a plain old man, Inspector. He wore old clothes and he looked like he was a hundred years old." Her temper had taken over, and Caywood hoped it would loosen the floodgates. She went on, now red in the face, "He was a nuisance. He looked like a beggar, and he acted like one." Then she realised what she had said. She pulled her smock sleeves down and pushed her glasses back farther on her nose. Caywood knew that the conversation had ended and that Mrs. Peters didn't feel kindly toward Quentin Stanley.

Caywood tipped his cap and then tugged it down close to his cold ears. He took one of the twelve self-allotted cigarettes out of the silver case in his right jacket pocket. He puffed hard on the cigarette as the wind blew and whistled around him. There was an irregular stone path extending the full length of cottage row. Melting snow made the path treacherous, and now slush flung up from the road added to the mess that Caywood slid through. Cheamley was everywhere white, wet, splattered, and quiet as St. Mary's Church. He passed a vacant cottage and knocked on the door of the next, waited, and knocked harder. The cottage looked like all the rest. It was yellow-gray stone with two windows in the front separated by a central door that opened not more than two feet from the road. The roof pushed down on walls and gave the appearance of flattening the cottage into the landscape.

The door cracked. Caywood tossed a half-finished cigarette into the road. He looked at his list and then spoke to the face peering through the crack.

"Mrs. Gill, I'm Detective Chief Inspector Caywood. I've come to talk to you about your neighbor, Quentin Stanley. May I come in? Frightfully cold."

Grudgingly, she cracked the door a bit more. "Please don't track snow in."

Caywood scraped his boots as dutifully as any schoolboy. She closed the door quickly behind him.

"Cold, don't you know."

"Heard you the first time, Inspector." She was wrapped in two old sweaters, one striped blue, the other green. Two buttons were missing, but a large pin held the cardigans tight around her wrinkled neck. Her hair was white, straight, and held up on the left side by a blue plastic barrette that she probably had treasured from childhood.

The room was neat, and as full of bric-a-brac as Stanley's had been bare. Shelf upon shelf lined the walls of her front room. There was a single log burning in the grate, together with some mouldy old paper that gave the room an odor of dead mice. Then Caywood realised that the stacks of books and newspapers throughout the room served a purpose other than reading.

"May I sit down, please?" Caywood held his cap in his left hand.

"Yes, of course." She cleared a torn brown leather chair, and he sat on the broken spring as carefully as possible.

"When did you last see Quentin Stanley?"

"Haven't seen him in years," Charlotte Gill replied.

"Years, Mrs. Gill? He was your neighbor, and Cheamley is not exactly a metropolis." Caywood was astonished.

"I rarely go out, only to the greengrocer's and butcher every two weeks."

He thought her pension must be terribly small. The lady was

quite thin, with frail arms and knobby, arthritic fingers. He noticed her legs now. Thick white cotton stockings, too large to stay up on such thin legs, ballooned around her ankles. Her feet were stuck in white canvas shoes.

"I never have visitors," she confessed as the silence of the room embarrassed her. "I have no friends since George died."

"When did that happen?"

"Twenty years ago, when he came home from the war. Maybe it was longer. My memory's going these days."

"I'm sorry, Mrs. Gill." He paused, then, "Did you ever see Mr. Stanley on the road?"

"A long time ago. We did not go out at the same times."

Caywood gave up, but tried to be pleasant. "You have quite a collection of magazines and paperbacks."

"Mrs. Peters brings them to me. Very nice lady, she is."

"Gives you all the remainders?"

"Yes, they won't give her money back, so she gives them to me."

"Well, if you haven't seen Mr. Stanley recently, maybe you can tell me where you were Wednesday night?"

"In my bed where I should be, and don't ask me if I can prove it."

Caywood grinned and tipped his hat as he let himself out the door. "Thank you, Mrs. Gill."

Looking around, he saw that the public house was now open and strode toward it.

The Angels in Green Inn was old enough to have provided Elizabeth I with refreshment. The inn was the second building established in Cheamley, and when Caywood saw it wallowing in its authentic antiquity and current state of decay, he knew his visit would be the third mistake of the day. Although the morning was clear and somewhat warmer, snow clung for its life to the thatched roof of the inn. It carpeted the cobblestones and draped the hedges that separated the building from the road and kept the inebriated from rolling into the river.

The yellow stone building rose two storeys under its thatch with great windows stretching in banks of three on either side of the green door. The lower storey, blackened by centuries of soot and pollution that filtered through the hedges, framed the windows and enhanced the stained glass at the top of each set of windows. Caywood could not understand why the stained glass panels of angels were on the front of a public house. Yet there they were, on either side of the door, together with the arms of England.

"What a muddle," Caywood muttered as he went through the heavy green door. Glancing up at the massive oak beams, he sensed the weight and age of them and the history of this place. A great stone fireplace dominated the room. Here again were tiles of green angels framing the grate where logs crackled and spat. The brilliant glow penetrated the dark corners and reflected off the polished bar onto the rows of sparkling glasses behind it.

Finally, Caywood saw Harry Kirk sitting next to a tortoiseshell cat on a bench beside the fireplace. The red velvet covering of the long seat had lost its nap, and shiny spots reflected the flames of the fire. Caywood sat beside his sergeant and faced the worn oak table that was immediately in front of them.

"Who's your friend?" Caywood patted the cat, who conspicuously ignored him.

"She got here first. Comes with the fire, I believe."

"Well, it's started off all wrong, Harry. Those two old ladies don't know anything, and even if they do, they're not saying anything."

"Which ones?"

"Violet Peters, the newslady, and Charlotte Gill, who is in the next cottage. How did you make out?"

"No better, but at least there's a list of all the inhabitants and here's a map of the area."

"Have you ordered?"

"Not yet."

"See if you can get us some coffee. Maybe they serve it."

"Right."

Sergeant Kirk, knowing his duties well, fetched one white, one black, and some dreadful rolls.

Caywood looked at the list. "One of us has to return to question Alfred Peters this afternoon. He and the missus have shifts. You might try to get more out of Mrs. Gill than I did. Put on your charm, Harry, and try her."

"She's the village recluse, according to Vicar," Kirk said. "Says she barely comes out, and then only for food."

Caywood offered a piece of roll to the cat. She flicked a disdainful look in his direction.

"She belongs here, Inspector. She knows."

"I suggest we avoid this place in the future," Caywood advised. "The empty car park should have been the warning."

Caywood took another swallow of coffee. "How's the home front?"

"Sorry you asked," Kirk said. "Angela's still making noises about a divorce. Says I'm never home and that I pay more attention to my work than I do to her."

"Sounds like she's taking lessons from Miss Eliza Crisp. Sorry to hear it, Harry. Keep trying. Maybe we can get through early tonight."

They left the pub. "I'll keep on with the row of cottages and try to do better," Caywood said.

"Right you are, Inspector."

"I'll continue down the left side of the road and meet you at the church at about three."

"Let's make it four. Maybe Vicar will offer tea."

"What a rascal you are, Harry."

Caywood saw a wrinkled face peek through the curtains as he walked up to the cottage next to Charlotte Gill's. The cottages were all cold yellow-gray stone, darkened by the years of road traffic splatting them. He wondered how each family arrived at the correct one in the dead of night. He knocked on the door of the third cottage and looked at the list Kirk had given him.

"Mrs. Weller?" Caywood tipped his cap.

"Miss Weller," she corrected.

He could see that she was in a wheelchair. "Detective Chief Inspector Peter Caywood here, Miss Weller. May I come in?"

She hesitated and finally opened the door to her parlor, which was as neat as Mrs. Gill's was cluttered.

"I've come to ask you about Mr. Quentin Stanley." He noticed that her pale hands began to twitch nervously. She coughed but made no effort to speak as she wheeled her chair around with great precision.

"Miss Weller, did you hear what I said?"

"Yes, of course I did. Sit down, Inspector." She pointed to a rose-flowered chintz sofa that Caywood thought was too attractive for a Cheamley cottage on this side of the road. The fragrance of coffee and cinnamon filled the room. He wished he had some of whatever the lady had in the kitchen to overcome what he'd drunk at The Angels.

"Thank you." He brought out his notebook. "Mr. Stanley died Wednesday night between ten-thirty and midnight. Can you tell me where you were?"

"Right here, locked in this chair, Inspector."

"Yes, I understand. How long have you been confined to a chair?" he asked as pleasantly as possible.

"My back was broken ten years ago, and I've been in it ever since. The curse of my life," she added sullenly.

Her legs were covered by a blanket, so he could not verify her story by the presence of atrophied muscles. He had been caught by the wheelchair routine as a young detective sergeant and vowed he never would be again.

"Did you know Quentin Stanley?"

"Yes, he did heavy cleaning for me every month."

"You live by yourself?"

"Yes. I do now. My mother died two years ago. We were able to look after ourselves with Mr. Stanley's help."

"What day of the month did Mr. Stanley come?"

"Usually the fourth Thursday."

"And what did he do?"

"Mopped, dusted, turned the mattress, beat the rugs. Carried any heavy trash to the pit."

"That's quite a lot. How long did he stay on the days he came?"

"Half a day. That's all I could afford." In spite of her ready reply, she seemed preoccupied.

"How much did you pay him?"

"One pound ten, far more than he deserved."

The longer Hazel Weller talked, the more Caywood appreciated her self-reliance. There was a small fire in the grate that made her room more comfortable. Small logs were easily available to her immediately next to the grate. Long matches were on her right. There was some kind of contraption that caught the ashes. Caywood noticed that the lady had strong arms and large shoulders. She looked well fed. Her sweater was clean, neatly buttoned, and without a single patch. Hazel Weller obviously took good care of herself and her environment.

"Did you like Mr. Stanley?"

"I appreciated him."

"That's not what I asked," he persisted. "Did you like him?"

"Not particularly. He was a quiet, drab, sad man. Never had much to say."

"Was he married?"

"Not to my knowledge."

Caywood pulled out the picture of a child he had found in Stanley's house.

"Have you ever seen this child in this village?"

She took it and pulled some tortoiseshell-framed glasses from her right sweater pocket. "No, I don't remember seeing anyone like this. It's an old photo, isn't it?"

"Yes, appears to be. Do you know Mrs. Gill?"

"Barely see her."

"She doesn't visit you?"

"No, never. Stays to herself."

"Did Quentin Stanley work for her?"

"He never said. I never asked."

"I should have known," Caywood muttered under his breath.

"Do you ever get to the news kiosk, Miss Weller?"

"No. Occasionally Mrs. Peters will bring me a magazine or a paperback."

"One more question. When was the last time you saw Quentin Stanley?"

"I don't remember precisely, but I suppose it was the last time he worked here. I appreciated Quentin for what he did, though he was well paid. Frankly, I don't know what I'm going to do."

For the first time, Hazel Weller's defenses began to fall.

"Who will help me?"

"Is there no one else in the village who will help?" Caywood asked.

"Only Walter Thompson, and frankly, Inspector, he's not trustworthy, at least in my opinion."

Caywood felt sorry for her. She sat there, a mousy-haired lady, every hair in place, bright pink rouge on her pale face. Her hands lay quietly folded across her lap now. Her worry and despair were obvious. Resignation eased up from her hands to her face and wiped away her winkles. Her face went blank. She said nothing else. Caywood let himself out.

Caywood passed the Thompson cottage after he had knocked several times. Old John Riley poked his head out the door to check on the noise.

"They're not at home," he shouted. "The mister and missus work, and the children are at school." He shut the door firmly.

When Caywood knocked on his door, the old man was about to shout again when he saw the tall, sandy-haired man looking down on him.

"Detective Chief Inspector Caywood, Rumsden CID. I'm here to talk to you about Quentin Stanley."

"Who?"

Caywood repeated himself, shouting as loudly as he could.

"Why didn't you say so? Come in. Come in."

"What's the noise, John?" An elderly woman with hennaed hair came into the room.

"I'm Detective Chief Inspector Caywood, investigating the death of Quentin Stanley."

"Sit down, Inspector," she said. "John, move some of your things. There, there you are, Inspector. Have a seat. Don't mind John." She touched a finger to the side of her head several times to indicate eloquently the state of her husband's mind.

Caywood nodded.

John sat in another of the three overstuffed chairs that faced the fireplace. A rather small log spat and crackled in the grate.

"Now, tell us what happened to poor Quentin," the woman said as she sat next to Caywood.

"You are?" Caywood hesitated.

"Oh, bless you." She smiled a row of ancient teeth. "I'm Pauline Riley and that's my husband, John."

Caywood smiled. "Did you know Quentin well?" He checked the list Kirk had given him.

"Oh no. No one knew Quentin well. Kept to himself, he did."

"What did he say?" John Riley asked.

"Wants to know about Quentin. Let me talk to the Inspector, John. Read a book, why don't you?"

Caywood was grateful. "Thank you, Mrs. Riley. Did either of you see Quentin last night?"

"No, we were here last night. Quentin works for many people in the village, but we take care of ourselves. Works for Miss Weller. Don't know what the poor soul will do now," she rambled on.

"Did you see any of your neighbors last night?" Caywood persisted.

"No, we had supper, and I washed up. We listened to the radio and went to bed."

"Didn't hear any unusual noises?"

"No, I didn't, and John doesn't pay attention."

Caywood appreciated her frankness. He pulled the photo out. John Riley took it quickly, without being asked, in an effort to make up for being left out of the conversation.

"Has either of you ever seen this child?" Caywood asked.

"No," she said as her husband shook his head. "Queer-looking thing, isn't he? But a happy smile on his face."

"One of them Chinese children," John Riley decided.

"Oh, I know," Mrs. Riley said. "Not Chinese, mongoloid, but I don't know him."

"Same thing," Riley decided. "Chinese in Cheamley?" He laughed a silly giggle.

"Thank you very much for your help," Caywood said. "If you think of anything that might help clear up this matter, please telephone this number." Caywood handed her a vellum card.

"We certainly will," she assured him, and escorted him to the door.

Dustman to Ashes

With a second "thank you" Caywood was back in the road and about to knock on the next door. Mrs. Riley opened her door.

"You're wasting your time, Inspector. No one else at home in this row. All at work, they are."

Caywood tipped his cap and decided it was a rotten day. The heavens were about to open up again. The whole sky had turned from blue to gray and was now darkening even more. Off in the distance he saw snow sheeting down in the hills. He walked toward the pub for a little comfort. He decided to ring up Eliza. She did not answer.

Detective Sergeant Harry Kirk waited to question pub owner Nigel Martin later at a more appropriate time, appropriately late enough to talk casually over a pint of whatever Martin considered his best. He started with the shops, which included a greengrocer, butcher, tea shop, and finally the chemist's.

The cold did not bother Kirk. He considered himself a robust, healthy male, younger than his chronological years, and he felt a little more smug each time he saw his superior shiver. He strolled to the greengrocer's and peered through the window at the winter crop of vegetables. There were no customers when Kirk went in.

"Mr. O'Leary?" he asked of the only individual in the shop.

"Yes, I'm Dan O'Leary."

"Mr. O'Leary, I'm Detective Sergeant Harry Kirk from the Rumsden CID. Did you know the late Quentin Stanley?"

"Oh yes, he bought vegetables here."

"Did you see him Tuesday or Wednesday?"

"No. He came in Mondays as a rule."

Kirk found a yellow apple and put some brass on the counter. O'Leary indicated that there was no charge. Kirk polished the apple on his coat sleeve. He took a great bite that let juice run down his chin. He whipped out a large white handkerchief and cleaned up the mess. O'Leary stood quietly and smiled as Kirk swabbed the sticky apple juice out of his beard.

The greengrocer was a short, thin man who was clean-shaven as well as bald. He had given up on the compromise of a beard long ago but understood the sergeant's pride in all that hair.

"Did Mr. Stanley seem his usual self?"

"Same as usual."

"What was he like, Mr. O'Leary?"

"An average-size man. Very quiet, rarely said much. Bought only the necessities, paid for them, and went directly home."

"Did you like him? Were you friends?"

"There wasn't much to like or to dislike. He was a customer. Nothing more."

"Did he have any friends or relatives?"

"None that I know of."

"Where were you Wednesday night?"

"Here, in the back room going over my supplies and accounts."

"Was anyone with you? What time did you leave for home?"

"I took the last bus at about ten twenty-five. I was alone all evening."

"Where do you live?"

"Not far, in Collier. I have another shop there. My brother manages it."

"Did you see or hear anything unusual?"

"No. No one was in the road. I was the last one on the bus. Mr. Peters closed the kiosk as the bus left."

"Thank you very much, Mr. O'Leary. If you think of anything else that might be useful, please ring up our centre in the church hall or Rumsden CID." Kirk pulled a card from his wallet and handed it to him.

He considered buying some apples and oranges to take home to Angela, but thought better of it and walked out onto the edge of the road. When he looked at his watch, he knew it was time to meet the inspector. He unbuttoned his jacket and let the wind blow against his chest. He smiled just for a second, thinking of Caywood.

"Have you felt like a stranger in your own land?" Caywood asked as Kirk approached. He noticed the open jacket flapping in the wind, but did not comment.

"Yes, these old folk are an absolute closed circle. They are all recluses, tight-mouthed."

"I gather Stanley was a silent gnome who did their work and hobbled off at night to his hovel."

"They didn't like him," Kirk said.

"They didn't really dislike him either. So we have a rabbit of a man about whom no one had any enthusiasm but who was murdered. Isn't it interesting? Nobody except Mrs. Shaw, so far, seems to care if he's dead. 'So what?' they seem to be saying, except for one wheelchair lady Weller who essentially says, 'What am I to do without him?' Quiet, unassuming, drab people are all too frequently extraordinarily devious. They hide a great deal behind those quiet facades. Quentin Stanley was not murdered by accident. He was not a thief or surely we would have found some hint of it. So why was he killed, Harry?"

"Blackmail?"

"Well, that's as good a motive as I can think of for the present."

"I'm willing to work on that theory until something better suggests itself," Kirk said.

"Unless, of course, the whole village was being blackmailed, and they did him in en masse."

"He was in an excellent position to know much about many."

"Yes, right. Shouldn't you button your jacket, Harry? A mite cold out here."

"Good fresh air. Cleans out your lungs. Better than those cigs of yours."

"Cleans out my lungs very well, Sergeant. My first morning cigarette brings up a lovely oyster of phlegm, and thereafter my bellows pump and blow without problem."

Kirk felt nauseous and began to feel a chill. "I believe it's an appropriate hour to call on the vicar. I don't recommend the cake."

Caywood smiled and rang the rectory bell.

The housekeeper, Mrs. Shaw, made a ceremony of looking at her pendant watch when she saw who was at the door. She ushered them in.

"Come in, Inspector, Sergeant," Vicar Morgan invited. "Just in time for tea."

"That would be very nice indeed," Caywood said.

Kirk sneezed as if to add an exclamation point to Caywood's acceptance.

"Excuse me." Kirk grabbed his handkerchief.

"All that clean air, Harry?"

"Sit down, gentlemen." Morgan put another log on the fire. "Sit close to the fire, Sergeant."

Kirk did so, much to his embarrassment.

Caywood looked around the study again and assessed it to be one that belonged to a true scholar. Books dominated the room, piled on the desk, beside it, and on shelves that extended from floor to ceiling. The fireplace hearth of mottled green-and-white tiles spread out three feet in front of the quiet, glowing embers. An engraving in a great gilt frame filled the space above the fireplace. A few small logs were stacked on the hearth. The one window was hung with heavy green velvet draperies. The vicar's desk faced the fireplace but was separated from it by a green leather sofa and two huge brown chairs that Caywood remembered. The essence of the room was that of coolness, neatness. The furniture was clean, in good repair, yet there was an air of shabby gentility.

The housekeeper rolled in the tea trolley. Kirk gave Caywood the high sign when he spied the leftover cake awaiting another victim.

Vicar Morgan poured much-appreciated cups, which he refilled twice while the cake gathered more dust.

"Vicar," Caywood asked, "did Quentin Stanley work in the church?"

"The heavy work, once a week."

"Did you know him very well?"

"No, not very. He was a quiet man. Did his work, said nothing."

Caywood produced the picture of the child. "Ever see this before?"

"No, I don't think so." The vicar put on his steel-framed glasses and looked closely. "This is an old photograph."

"Yes."

"Of a mongoloid child."

"So it would appear. Whose child?"

"To my knowledge there has never been such a child in Cheamley. Did you find this at Stanley's?"

Caywood nodded.

"Probably a relative's child."

"Stanley never married?"

"He came home from the war and never married. He went off a bachelor and stayed one."

"Where were you Wednesday night, Vicar?"

Morgan smiled. "As I told you, Altar Society is Wednesday nights, and there were various committee meetings and choir practice."

"Can you remember who else was there, Vicar? Miss Weller, Mrs. Peters, Mrs. Gill, were they there?"

"They don't belong to Altar Society."

"When did the meeting begin and end?"

"Oh, shortly after seven-thirty. I was in and out. Usually ends about ten-fifteen. We have some members who take the last bus to Collier."

"Which leaves . . ."

"About ten twenty-five, thereabouts. The driver knows who he brought, so he will wait for a straggler."

"Same driver?" Kirk asked.

"No, they vary, but the bus travels in a circuit, so whoever the driver was that night knew who'd come. The ladies boarded the bus at Collier, traveled to Rumsden, on around the loop to Cheamley. We have church members in Collier, Rumsden, Brewdon, and Wateson as well."

"You are a very popular vicar to have church members from such distances." Kirk was impressed.

"We're the only church, Sergeant. Has nothing to do with me. If there were churches in those villages, then I would go to them. It's because of our physical plant that they come," Morgan said.

"And they all support St. Mary's financially?"

"Yes, most of them do."

"And if they didn't?"

"Then I would be transferred by the bishop, to answer your next question. Yes, we all work hard to keep St. Mary's in the black," Morgan said and offered Kirk some cake.

He declined.

"The church is lovely, Vicar," Caywood observed, "a tribute to your faithful."

Kirk handed the vicar a copy of the list he'd made for himself and the inspector.

"Would you mind placing the village name next to the appropriate names on the list?" Caywood asked. "That would save a good bit of time."

"Of course."

"Can you think of any reason why someone would want to kill Quentin Stanley?"

"No. I've wondered about that. He was the sort of man who faded into the walls. He never offended anyone."

"He offended someone," Caywood said. "Thank you for the tea, Vicar. We'll probably have to come back, but I promise not to impose."

"You're truly welcome."

"And thank you for the use of the church hall for our information area."

"Yes, sir." Kirk sneezed. "Excuse me."

"Trust you're not coming down with something, Sergeant," the vicar said.

Caywood smiled, buttoned his coat, and pulled his cap down as they walked outside. Kirk sneezed again.

"Button your jacket, Harry. I'm not impressed with your nonsense."

When Caywood reached his office in Rumsden the following morning, he learned that Kirk had called in sick. He was not surprised, but the idea of slogging about alone made him weary before he began. This was a dreary case with drab, dull people who were so caught up in their inconsequential lives they did not care that one of them had been brutally murdered. He decided to see Quentin Stanley's cottage again and complete the questioning in the village.

Out in the car park, he greeted the sunshine with the best smile he had. Smoking the second cigarette of the day, he rolled his car out onto the road. Sunlight bounced on the snow-lined road and lit up Caywood's sandy hair, outlining the permanent wrinkles on his face. The wind blew out his cigarette, to his disgust, and he dispersed the smoke through the cracked window. He flicked the ash from his brown silk tie and tried to concentrate on the road and Rumsden traffic. As he maneuvered through the trucks and autopool drivers, he reached into his case for another cigarette. The third of the day and only nine left. He took a long drag and let the smoke course slowly, deeply through his lungs and out his nose and into the air above his head. What a glorious taste.

He parked the car in front of Quentin Stanley's and tossed the last four millimeters of his most recent cigarette into the snow. The key was on a long nylon cord marked "Cheamley." He let himself into the cottage, went into the bedroom, pushed the old blue blankets aside, sat and thought. His eyes scanned the room, up from the floor to the ceiling, back down again. Round and round the room his eyes went. What a damned boring, unrewarding job this is, he thought. He ought to marry Eliza and live on her money, except that she refused. At least he teased her about it.

He went into the bathroom, checked the taps, got down on all fours and flashed his torch through the centuries of dirt under the bathtub. Amazing, he thought. Stanley was a cleaner for hire and couldn't do the least job in his own house.

Caywood decided he was wasting valuable time and made up his mind to try again another day. He knew there had to be more to a man's life than what he had found here.

With one more look in the kitchen, he hoped the hour would not be a total loss. The kettle still held water. There were no electrical appliances, and Caywood wondered where Stanley got ice for his old-fashioned icebox. He opened it to the stench of rotting meat and green-layered cheese. He closed it quickly and looked in the top, where ice should have been. There it was, perhaps the first clue to this poor man's life, a heavy brown envelope tied with sturdy cord.

The whole upper chest of the antique wooden icebox was gray and black with mould and mildew. The envelope fitted exactly, and Caywood had to squeeze a long finger down and under one edge. He worked it up, trying desperately not to tear or damage the dark brown envelope, which was sprinkled with dirt and roach droppings. Caywood shook it clean and deposited it in a large plastic bag in his car.

Well, he thought, that's the best poor man's safe I've seen.

He drove over the north bridge and on impulse suddenly turned left onto the older road to Rumsden. There would be less traffic this time of day, he reasoned. He knew it would be ten minutes longer, but the scenery was worth it. Even in winter the limestone skeleton of this part of the earth pushed through the snow. This was where the pasque flowers would bloom in April, if April ever came. And if May followed, the yellow archangel would flower, and then the land would turn purple again with the woolly thistle. The tree creeper, inhabitant of the local woodland, would begin its high-pitched siren's song to insects in the trees. This would not begin until February. And now it was November. Caywood came back to reality, gave up his reluctance to get back to Rumsden, and pushed the car along the curved road that plowed through country woods. He put the woolly thistle away until summer and considered brandy all the way home.

Rumsden CID stood like a sentinel at the corner of Queens Road and Cable Street. The facade, of airly recent vintage, was of yellowstone hiding an ancient building riddled by decay. There were three storeys, with holding cells at the lowest level and more cells and working police on the middle level. Records dating back to the first police constable in Rumsden were stored at the top of the building. Spontaneous combustion was not confined to the top floor; it occurred with some degree of regularity in Caywood's office.

He put the car in his assigned space and went up the rear steps into the long hallway that extended from one end of the building to the other. His office was the largest one and farthest away from the centrally located duty sergeant's desk.

"Chief Inspector Caywood there, please?"

"Not in yet." The duty sergeant held the phone.

"This is Kirk. Tell him that—"

"Hold on, Harry, he's coming in now," the duty sergeant said and turned to Caywood. "For you, Chief Inspector."

"Right, take it in my office, please."

Caywood threw his overcoat on the brass rack just inside his office door and gingerly placed Quentin Stanley's envelope in the center of his black steel desk.

"That you, Kirk? What's going on with you? . . . That bad, eh? Well, I need you here, Sergeant, but I don't want you sneezing and spewing all over me. . . . Very well, do try to get in here Monday. I'm twenty-four hours behind now." Caywood replaced the receiver. He buzzed for the duty sergeant. "Howell, is Allen in the lab?"

"Yes."

"Any messages for me from the police surgeon?"

"No."

"Cheery soul, Howell is," Caywood muttered as he strode to the lab. The place was not the modern, gleaming place of science depicted in the cinema or on television. The police laboratory was a set of oak desks, stained, scarred, and paper-laden. A long table that was divided by a center sink into work spaces on either side was just as old as the others, but a trifle neater.

"Allen," Caywood shouted into the laboratory. He heard a muffled reply from the darkroom. The wait was not long. He had already marked and made a list of the contents of the envelope, but he needed copies of some things and photos of others.

A fat young man with smelly brown hair emerged from the darkroom. "Inspector, what do you need?" The fellow's smock was pocked with acid holes scattered randomly over the front. A cigarette hung from the left side of his thick lips.

"I have an envelope here from the cottage of Quentin Stanley of Cheamley. We found his murdered body Thursday. This needs to be done very carefully, Allen, because thus far we are without a clue. I would like a detailed report as early as possible, like this afternoon. Copies of everything."

Allen lit another cigarette from the one already burning and grunted. "Do my best."

"All I expect," Caywood said, "and please do be careful." He returned to his office.

"Howell, please come in here. I'm shorthanded today."

"Yes, sir."

"Here's a list of men and women who live in Cheamley. Please check each for previous marriages, for Army or Navy service, etc. Start as soon as you can. I'm going back to the village now. I'll be back before tea, I hope."

Caywood took the quick route back to Cheamley. Leaving his car at the pub, he walked to the small thatched cottage close to The Angels in Green.

The cottage belonged to Paul Adams, father of the two children who had found Quentin Stanley's body. Caywood rang the bell and waited. A boy of about ten years, with curly red hair and great blue eyes, opened the door.

"Hello, are you Derek?"

"Yes," he said hesitantly to the tall stranger.

"I am Detective Chief Inspector Caywood. Will you tell your mother that I am here?"

Caywood heard the boy run through the house shouting for "Mum."

"Mrs. Adams? Detective Chief Inspector Caywood. I'm here to talk to the children about Quentin Stanley."

"Come in, please."

Caywood carried his cap in his hand and walked through a pleasant hall filled with dried-flower arrangements on lovely tables and family portraits on light-painted walls. She led him into an airy lounge. The rear wall was three windows in a line; rising above and in front of oak paneling were two white wicker chairs with plump green and yellow cushions.

Mrs. Adams stood in front of the stone fireplace. "Please sit down, Inspector."

He chose the green-leafed sofa, and she sat across the coffee table from him on a small delicate gold chair.

"Derek," she called, "please find Rose and bring her here. Hurry, now." She turned to Caywood. "They are terribly frightened still, Inspector. We had to have the doctor in. Both have had night terrors, and they won't eat."

"I'm so sorry, Mrs. Adams. This has been a dreadful experience for them, I know. I promise to be as brief as possible. You have my word."

They came in quietly and went to their mother. She held them close. "Inspector Caywood wants to ask you about what happened the other night."

"He was dead," Derek blurted out.

"Yes, I know, Derek. What I want to know is, what time were you in the churchyard?" Caywood saw Rose's face begin to flush. "Now, Rose, please don't cry. I'm not here to upset you. I need your help in solving this case."

"Rose, please don't fret. Tell Inspector Caywood what happened Thursday."

"I'll tell," Derek interrupted.

"That's a good boy." His mother kissed his forehead.

"My sister and I left school and decided to cross the road to the church."

"Which was very naughty and forbidden," their mother said.

"Ah," Caywood observed, "forbidden lark and now punished for their sin by finding Quentin Stanley. The same thing always happened to me, Derek," he confessed. "Every time I did something I wasn't supposed to, the good Lord reached down and whispered in my mother's ear."

Mrs. Adams looked horrified.

"However, I must say, this was a dreadful thing to happen to you."

"Worse for poor Quentin." Rose had finally found enough courage to speak.

"Yes, quite worse," Caywood said most sympathetically. "Were you playing?" he asked the children.

"Yes," Rose said. "We crossed the road because we heard there was a bear hibernating in a cave beyond the church. He lives in Mayfest."

Caywood smiled.

Mrs. Adams looked like she would faint. "Rose, don't you or

Derek ever do such a thing again. You will be punished severely. There's no cave around Cheamley."

"Rose, my dear," Caywood said, "there are no bears in this area. Someone was teasing you."

"Quentin told us," she said almost defiantly, "and he lives in Cheamley. He should know."

"Rose, mind your manners, please." Her mother gave her a little tap on her arm. Then she looked really distressed. "Oh, Inspector, you don't suppose he said that to . . ."

Caywood read her thoughts. "Mrs. Adams, there is absolutely no sign that Stanley was that sort, really."

"What a relief!"

"What are you talking about?" Derek asked. "Quentin did *so* say there was a bear in the woods."

Before Mrs. Adams could speak, Caywood asked, "Did Quentin talk to you and Rose frequently?"

"Of course. Every time he came to clean he talked to us. He loved us, didn't he, Rose?"

"Yes, he said all the time that we were good children and kind to him."

"Apparently Quentin was very lonely," Caywood said to the children. "Were you with him on Wednesday?"

"No, he worked at the Grants' in Mayfest that day. Mrs. Grant worked him very hard, he used to say," Derek volunteered.

"That's why we were so surprised to see him there," Rose spoke up.

"Did he speak to you when you found him?"

"No, he didn't." Rose began to cry. "He had blood all over his head. He didn't even move."

"What did you do?" Caywood asked.

Derek said, "I said his name over and over again, but he didn't move, so we ran to the vicar's."

"And then?"

"I told him where Quentin was," Rose said.

"Then they came home once Vicar Morgan rang the police," Mrs. Adams said.

"Did you see anything else?" Caywood asked.

"No," Derek said.

"It got too cold, and the snow came down harder, so we had to leave," Rose said.

"Did you see anything else at all?" Caywood asked.

Derek looked at Rose just for a split instant before he said no.

"No," Rose added.

The glance between the children worried him. Caywood decided to try again later.

CHAPTER 4

A Little Help from the Girls

"Are you ready, Eliza?"

"Depends."

"On what, pray tell?" Caywood asked.

"Where are you taking me?"

"I have some work to catch up on, so I thought, we might go to Charlie's for an early dinner. I have a ticket for a play for you."

"By myself? Are you serious?"

"Course I am. I'll take you to the theatre and pick you up after for a drink."

"You are serious, aren't you, Peter?"

"Absolutely. What's wrong with a liberated woman going to the theatre by herself?"

"I think you're right," she agreed too quickly. "Besides, I might find something worthwhile at the play."

"There you are. I knew I couldn't keep a good girl down."

"I'll be ready in a minute. Fix us a sherry, please."

"Eliza?"

"Yes, Peter."

"Please don't wear the tiara tonight. We're running a bit late."

"As you wish, my dear. Wouldn't go with this outfit anyway." She came into the room in a lovely electric blue velvet suit. She took a sherry from Caywood and kissed him. He put his arms around her and kissed back.

"Enough of that. You promised me a night out." She swallowed the sherry and handed him her coat to carry. "Have you seen my bag? Ah, here it is. Let's go."

They were seated at a decent table at Charlie's twenty minutes later. The smell of sauces wafted toward them. "What would you like?" Caywood asked as she scrutinized the menu.

"A small fillet and some glazed potatoes and a green salad and coffee."

"Sounds good," Caywood said. "We'll both have that," he said to a bored waiter.

"Do you wish to see the wine list?" the waiter asked.

"No, thank you," Caywood tried to push the waiter on his way. "And make the fillets rare."

"Yes, sir."

"Surly lot, waiters," he said loud enough for the man to hear.

She laughed. "Just for that you will eat burned meat after he dumps the potatoes in your lap."

He offered her a cigarette.

"Am I to deprive you?" she asked. "Never mind then."

She noticed for the first time that his hair was grayer than she remembered. Maybe she had taken him so for granted that she had stopped noticing. There were a few more wrinkles around his mouth, but his eyes were as steel blue and sparkling as ever. He was on the downhill side of forty but still acted, at times, like her adolescent nephew. When he looked as tired as he did tonight she wished he'd quit and help her manage Crisp's.

"So many things to do," he raised his voice above the piano in the bar close to them. "Because Harry's out sick, and I'm quite behind in this case."

"What's wrong with Sergeant Kirk?"

"Some kind of respiratory thing. He walks around with his coat open in the middle of a snowstorm. Makes me tired in more ways than one."

"Oh, macho, macho, Peter. He's trying to get under your skin. Someone's stepped on his masculine ego."

"It's Angela, I'm afraid. She's asking for a divorce."

"Well then, a cold and a few days at home may be what they both need."

Caywood smiled. "Touché. You're probably right, as usual."

"Is this a murder case?"

"Yes."

"Then there's no rush about it, is there, actually? If someone's dead, they are dead."

"The idea is to find the murderer as quickly as possible, my dear."

"Well now, there's the point, isn't it? They've already fled. So what's the great hurry? The whole business is nonsense. The deed's done. Take your time."

"We might find some clues, actually," he argued and tried to be patient.

"Bloody nonsense. Let me have another cigarette." She saw the look of deprivation speed across his face. "Heavens above! I'll pay you back."

The waiter returned with supper.

"I said rare!" Caywood protested.

"Oh, I beg your pardon, sir. I'll take it back." He served Eliza a beautiful steak.

"Go ahead. Eat while it's hot," he said. She smiled her "told you so" smile.

"What's the play?" she asked, sprinkling salt on her salad.

"Some American import about love and murder. I forget the name."

"Why can't I go with you and help you?"

"Out of the question," he said testily, turning around waiting for his steak.

"Open your mouth." She poked a potato into it. "I want to come. Please, Peter."

The waiter placed the same burned steak in front of him. Eliza smiled wickedly.

"I'll throw it at him," he hissed.

"Keep your voice low. That's what got you into trouble before."

"Not to worry, Miss Crisp. I'll have the last laugh." Caywood did not touch his steak, but when they were ready to leave he asked the waiter to wrap it up so he could take it to his cat. He paid the check, helped Eliza on with her coat, and ceremoniously placed ten pence on the table.

"You wouldn't," she whispered.

"I just did." He took her arm and they laughed all the way to his car.

"Please, Peter, let me go with you."

He reluctantly gave in.

When they arrived at Rumsden CID, he tried to make her comfortable in his spartan office. Their coats on the rack close to the door, Caywood pushed a chair close to the desk for her and bent a green lamp in her direction. He then tackled the package on his desk. It was a wire basket with all the material he had brought in from Quentin Stanley's cottage. On top was the dirty envelope he'd found in the icebox; attached to it was a report from P.C. Allen of the lab. In essence Allen said he had found nothing but mould, dirt, insect droppings, and Caywood and Stanley's fingerprints.

"Here, see what you can find in this." Caywood handed Eliza a small tan journal. She took her gloves off carefully and tossed them on the edge of the desk.

"What's this?" she asked.

"A notebook from the victim's cottage. Read it with a nose for anything out of the ordinary."

"Names and sums," she said after turning several pages.

"Go all the way through."

"Names and sums all the way through," she repeated.

"Any dates?" Caywood tried to ease the great brown envelope open.

"Yes. Dates, names, sums."

"Start with the first of this year," he instructed. "Find it?"

"Yes."

"Now, is there a pattern over a month's time?"

"You mean names and dates in certain sequences?"

"Yes." He got the envelope open and spread a sheath of documents and photos over the desk. He began a list with descriptive identification.

"Birth certificate for one Quentin Stanley. RAF papers for Stanley. Graduation from Cheamley School." He had just about reached the bottom of the stack. "What ho, Miss Crisp, the first break."

"What is it?"

"A birth certificate and baptism record for James Alexander Stanley. Must be for the child in the picture."

"When was he born?"

"It's in German," Caywood said.

"Well, can't you read it? Here, give it to me." She reached over the desk.

"It's from Munich, dated 1945. That can't be correct," she said.

"Why not?"

"Well, think, Peter. That was the end of World War II. Germany was destroyed. How could any official records be kept? There was no place to keep records in."

"You're correct. This must be some kind of forgery, but the date may be close. What did you find in the journal? Read out some of the names."

She flipped back to the page that began the year. "Weller, Sare, Vicar, Clemson, Adams."

"Yes, those are all Cheamley people."

"Is there a pattern?"

"Yes, here, see for yourself. He worked once a month for Weller, once a week for the vicar, once a week for Clemson, and so on."

She handed the book to him.

"Take a look at this picture and this one." He gave her the faded photographs.

"Mongoloid child, it looks like. Difficult to tell. I may be wrong, but it's the same child in both pictures. I would guess about five years apart."

"Why would Stanley have these pictures?"

"Because the baby is his child," Eliza said matter-of-factly. "Look here." She pointed out a sign in the background. "Air Force base somewhere."

"Right you are. It'll be enlarged first thing in the morning." He looked at his watch. "Time for a drink."

"And some food for you."

"I could use some, now that you mention it." He gingerly put everything in a great cardboard folder. He checked out for the night and drove to a pub several squares away from Headquarters.

"Do you think you can tolerate Rumsden's finest?" he asked.

"You're the one who's hungry. Anywhere suits at this hour."

The pub was crowded, and locals continued to push in although there was only an hour to closing. They sat at a tight corner table and waited to order.

"That's a strange lot you went through tonight," Eliza said.

"All from the victim's cottage. It is a motley mess that is leading me nowhere. The photographs will be the greatest help. Too bad Allen didn't blow them up the way he was told. Well, let's forget it."

They each had two drinks and some roast beef salad at the Rumsden Arms, and made their way out five minutes before closing.

"Will I see you tomorrow?" she asked as he opened the door to her flat.

"You saw what I'm up against." He kissed her. "I'll telephone tomorrow. We'll see."

On the following morning Caywood gave up his usual Sunday sleep-in and dragged himself to the office, where he found a snuffly-nosed recuperating Kirk. He gave him the material he and Eliza had been through the night before.

"Check out the certificate, Harry, and get a better enlargement of the boy. I'll be in Cheamley. Feel better, Harry?" He didn't wait for an answer.

After checking in at the temporary incident centre and depositing the most current information with them, he walked in the early-morning mist to the Clemson residence. It was a large, two-storey stone cottage surrounded by leafless, snow-festooned trees. A two-foot stone wall on either side enclosed an expanse of white blanket that in spring would be lovely green. He walked up three broad stone steps that led to the front door. It opened just as he rang the bell.

"I hope I won't detain you from church."

"I saw you coming up the walk, Inspector. I'm Caroline Clemson."

"How do you do, Mrs. Clemson?"

"Very well. Do come in. Everyone knows you're in the village."

She laughed. "My spies told me you were going around." Her speech was as rapid as an automatic gun.

She was an elderly, thin, white-haired lady dressed in a delicate rose-coloured cardigan, buttoned and topped off with a gold brooch. Her skirt was heavy gray tweed. She smiled and beckoned him in.

"Come in, come in. You must have some coffee with me and some breakfast, too, if you will."

"Oh no, thank you, Mrs. Clemson."

"Oh come on, Inspector." She led him into a breakfast room that was cheery although quite cold. The walls were a pale sky blue, and the table next to a window was covered with a white cloth. There were oak benches on either side. Caywood had taken off his cap, but he kept his tartan muffler around his neck, tucked into his reliable old jacket.

"White?" she asked. "There's sugar."

"Yes, please." He took the cup from her.

"Cinnamon toast in the oven." She didn't have to say it; he smelled the glorious aroma and began to feel warmer.

"Did you know Quentin Stanley?"

"Yes, of course, Inspector. He's cleaned this house for years. I've known Quentin since he was a child."

"Really?"

She put a plate of cinnamon toast in front of him and pointed to the grapefruit marmalade. "Yes, he sang in the church choir all his life—that is, until he returned from the war."

"I never would have believed that quiet, humble Quentin would have been a boy soprano."

"Quentin was like any other child in this village. Something happened during the war. I know that's too remote for you to consider."

"I don't know about that, Mrs. Clemson. Stanley was fifty years old when he died."

"And his parents were killed when he was fourteen, and he enlisted at fifteen. That was in 1940. Many boys lied about their ages. That was thirty-five years ago. You weren't even born, Inspector. Everything you know about that period has come from your school books."

He felt flattered, but didn't correct her. "Was he ever married or have any children?"

"I don't think so." She hesitated. "But really, I'm not certain. He was so sick when he came back. He was in the hospital for at least a year."

"Do you know why?" Caywood asked.

"I'm not sure, but malnutrition and probably his nerves."

"Do you think he may have been a prisoner of war? That's what's been going through my mind, particularly in light of what you've just said." Caywood pulled out some pictures and placed them on the breakfast table in front of Mrs. Clemson.

"Do you know this child?"

"Yes. I think that was Quentin's brother Ralph. The other child I do not know."

"Oh, I thought it was the same child," Caywood said.

"No," she replied.

"Where is the brother now?" Caywood asked.

"Oh, he died many years ago. You know mongoloid children do not have a normal life-span."

"Oh." Caywood's tone enforced his ignorance. "I'm having an enlargement made of the second photograph. I'll bring it back later. Was Quentin here on the day he died?"

"This past Wednesday? No, he usually was at the Sares' on Wednesday. Here on Mondays, the vicar's on Tuesdays. On Fridays he was at the Adamses'. Thursdays he rationed out to various and sundry."

"Are you sure about the Sares' on Wednesday?" Caywood asked. "I thought—" he paused and consulted his notes. "Ah, yes, here it is. The Adams children said Quentin worked for the Grants in Mayfest on Wednesday."

"Grants?" Mrs. Clemson looked quizzical. "I don't know them. Must be new people."

Caywood pushed back slightly from the table and looked at Mrs. Clemson. "My dear lady, would you like a job on the Rumsden CID? I'm short a sergeant now and you'd do splendidly."

"Inspector, there's nothing I'd like better. You must understand that I am bored to tears. I had led an active life until a year ago, when my bones gave out before I did. Believe me, my bones are eighty, my mind is nowhere near that. Truly, I am not a gossip. I'm just the oldest person in the village and I know the history of it and the people."

"Well, you have been of tremendous help to me, believe me, and I appreciate it."

"More toast?"

"No, thank you. I've had plenty. Delicious. I'd come daily if you'd let me."

"Your wife doesn't prepare breakfast?"

"Mrs. Clemson, you're too astute and observant for that. The word *bachelor* is engraved across my forehead."

"I'm afraid it is," she said.

Caywood noticed that she had a remarkably smooth face, which her smile lit up even more. Maybe because she acted so young, she looked so young. At last, there was someone in Cheamley who was likable.

Caywood swallowed the last bit of his coffee.

She rose slowly from her chair. "Takes a minute or two for the oil to start running to the moving parts," she said.

Caywood knew he'd found the grandmother he'd never known.

"By the way, Inspector, you must meet my son, Colin. He and Quentin were schoolboys together. Colin will be in later. He plays for all the churches in the area."

"Good," Caywood said. "That will be the best excuse I know to come back. Let me gather up a few more facts and let you tell me the truth about them."

She walked to the door with him.

"By the way, Mrs. Clemson, where were you Wednesday?"

"Playing the organ for the choir." She smiled. "We had a great crowd."

"Each supplying the other with an alibi," Caywood said. "Do you know the Adams children? They found the body. Said they'd been playing in the woods. What's in those woods to attract them, do you suppose?"

"Nothing in the woods, Inspector, but beyond the woods, just as you reach Mayfest, there's a marvelous sweet shop with all the chocolate any child could wish."

"You may have solved one of my problems, Mrs. Clemson. Thank you very much indeed."

He walked back to the church hall and fetched some cigarettes out of his car, parked far off the road. Voices and sweet music came through the old doors of St. Mary's as Caywood walked into the graveyard and beyond it into the woods. He took the path of least resistance, assuming the children had done the same. The first thing he found was a broken silver chain hanging on one of the lower branches. Snow had melted from the branches but it still clung to roots and ground. Caywood squatted down and brushed away all the snow and found nothing. He scraped some bark away, marked the naked trunk with a red pen, and walked on with the silver chain secure in his right jacket pocket. The woods were not dense, nor did they stretch on for miles. Where was Quentin killed? he asked himself. On the spot? Or close by? The greatest question was, Why did the murderer leave the body there?

Was he interrupted and had to flee? Was the body left there as a warning to others? Caywood walked on through the forest for a while. Then, quite suddenly, he was in Mayfest. The woods separated one world from another. The shops were closed as he walked along the High, but the sparkling bright color of them was inviting. The second shop on his left was Molly's Sweets. The window was done in silver and gold and made to look like a pirate ship with gold-foil-covered chocolate doubloons cascading from the ship toward the window. Caywood saw some leftover smudges from noses pressed to the glass. Such a place would have enticed any child, including Derek and Rose Adams, but he wondered if they had seen anything else.

He retraced his steps through the forest, finding nothing new, and got back to Cheamley. He walked down the road with a purpose. It was easy to do with wet cold freezing his face and reaching down to his bones. Caywood wanted it to be spring. Surely there would be flowers in this most desolate of villages.

When he finally reached his car, he lit up and decided his mind needed old Rumsden Road today.

The whole valley where he drove was a woodland interrupted here and there by villages, not unlike Cheamley, and threaded by the river that hemmed them in until it unraveled into the Thames. Where the Rumsden ran shallow near Stoneleigh Manor, the dippers, small birds, dove into the river and picked between pebbles and stones for food. These peculiar birds and gray wingtails frequent the valley, as do herons. He drove on and tried to get his mind back on murder. Instead he gave it up and went to his flat.

Caywood spent the rest of his Sunday there, walking about in the altogether, smoking and making lists. He felt that he knew very little about Quentin Stanley's murder, but what he did know was at least organised.

The kitchen was warm as he slapped his bare feet against the floor tiles and avoided the open window. It was a small though serviceable room, a stove with a kettle sitting on top like a monument, two chairs, a white table, and a refrigerator. The refrigerator was usually bare. The cabinets contained a motley assortment of twos—two saucers, two cups that didn't match, two plates that were chipped—and one water glass. Kirk saw it once, closed the doors, and called it Noah's ark. The sink was opposite the window, a fact he sometimes forgot as well as the spinster whose window and spyglass were across the courtyard. Caywood cursed and returned to the kitchen in rumpled underpants to finish tea and work on his notes. Two cups later, he and the papers went to the bedroom, where he decided Sunday was a day of rest. He wished Eliza were with him, but she couldn't be so he went to sleep.

CHAPTER 5

Where Are the Answers?

Vicar Morgan had set aside two large rooms together with an alcove for the police. It was at the rear of the church hall, near the back door. Caywood was grateful for the space and the tables and chairs that came with the accommodations.

When he strode into the church hall at 7 A.M. Monday and reached for the box on Quentin Stanley, he set it together with his briefcase on the table that was his desk at the incident centre.

"Sergeant Kirk here yet?" he asked P.C. Dexter.

"Not yet, sir, but he's expected."

"Please track down some coffee, will you, Dexter? The day is going to be long. Here's a list of people in the village that I want you to see. Ask the usual questions. Take careful notes and file them here by three o'clock this afternoon."

Dexter paled a bit and said, "Yes, sir, but we've done that."

"Do it again."

"Good morning, Inspector." Bareheaded, bald Harry Kirk arrived.

"Harry, in the Lord's name, why can't you keep a cap on your bald head in cold weather?"

"Yes, Inspector." The word *bald* cut.

Caywood looked at him again. "I'm glad you're back. Now, get that coffee Dexter is supposed to fetch and let's get started. He probably doesn't know where to look."

Kirk returned with two large china mugs and some biscuits on an ancient metal tray. They both sipped quietly for a few seconds. When he could no longer stand it, Caywood said, "Harry, it's

freezing in here. Please take my cap. I don't want you out anymore."

Kirk wrapped a muffler tighter around his neck. "Would you like
me to wear a shawl?"

"Never mind. Did you bring the photos and that birth certificate? What do you make of them? They came from Quentin
Stanley's."

"Yes, I brought them, but I didn't see anything important. Why
do you suppose he was murdered?" Kirk asked as he reached for a
biscuit.

"I suspect he had a secret life, or else he discovered someone
else's secret life. Somebody got mad enough to kill him. I think he
was a blackmailer. We have a great deal more legwork to do." He
looked at his sergeant, who began to shake with a chill. An explo-
sive cough followed. "For God's sake, Harry, go home. You'll con-
taminate us all. Get in bed and note any and all ideas you can
dream up in your delirium."

Kirk did not wait to be told twice. Caywood watched in disgust
as the still bareheaded Kirk went out into an extraordinarily cold
day.

Caywood gulped the remainder of his coffee and decided the
next one on his list would be the Sares. By now the children of
Cheamley were in the schoolyard throwing snowballs and getting
themselves miserably wet to start the day. He waved to Rose
Adams, who smiled at him as he crossed the yard and moved
across Back Green Road to the Sares'. The stone path had been
cleared from the front door, through the iron gate, on out to the
road. It was an imposing house that gave notice that someone
important lived here. The great thatched roof extended down,
surrounding the windows of the second storey like some loving
mother clasping and holding her young to her bosom.

There was a fleeting thought of Eliza as he rang the bell.

"Yes, sir?" She was rather thick in the middle, yet a neat young
woman with hair a little lighter than his, her face a bit more sullen.

"Detective Chief Inspector Peter Caywood. Are Mr. and Mrs.
Sare in, please?"

"I'll tell the missus you're here, sir."

She led him through the foyer into an elongated lounge that appeared cheerful and comfortable. He felt the warmth of the fireplace as he studied the bookshelves. They were orderly, though crammed. On the bottom shelf were several fancy cookbooks. Above them were old children's books, ragged, the spines torn and stained, attesting to their repeated use. He had just turned around when Mrs. Sare entered the room.

"Good morning, Inspector. I'm Sarah Sare. I'm sorry, my husband is at work. Please do sit down."

She was, to say the least, a beautiful woman, dark auburn hair to her shoulders, fair unblemished skin, and dressed in a fashionable azure frock that would have been more in place in London than Cheamley. Her voice was soft, and there was a whisper of a familiar perfume when she sat next to Caywood.

"How can I help you?" she asked.

"I'm investigating the death of Quentin Stanley. I believe he worked here the day he died."

"Yes, he did," she said. "He was here that day, but seemed perfectly well."

"Did he seem worried or concerned about anything?"

"No, if anything he seemed a little brighter and more cheerful than usual."

"What do you mean?" Caywood wondered.

"Well," she said, "Quentin was always a quiet sort, who said nothing even when you spoke to him. He smiled and said good morning to me that day. That's all."

"Did you notice anything else?"

"Not particularly. He had no personality or really anything to like. Please don't misunderstand me, Inspector. Quentin Stanley simply was not a friendly, likable person."

"Do you have children?"

"Yes, four. An older son who works in London and two younger boys; the middle boy is away at school, and the youngest, Knox, is still here with us, together with Hannah."

"Did Quentin get along well with Knox and Hannah?"

"As a matter of fact, he did. They were friends, I think. Quentin didn't seem to care if the children got underfoot."

"Was there anything unusual about Quentin or the last day he worked here? Anything that you can remember at all?"

She walked to the fireplace and prodded the logs to put out more heat. "Nothing unusual that I can think of offhand. Quentin asked if he could leave early. Had something he wanted to do."

"Did he leave early?"

"Yes, I believe he did, as a matter of fact."

"Did he say what he planned to do?"

"No, I don't remember that he did."

"May I speak to your maid? Was she here the day Quentin died?"

"Yes." Mrs. Sare rang for the maid. It was a tinkling little bell that had to be listened for to be heard.

"Yes, Mrs. Sare?" She appeared from nowhere.

"Kitty, Inspector Caywood wants to ask you some questions. Sit down and don't be afraid."

"Yes, Mrs. Sare," she replied.

"What is your full name?"

"Kitty Clarence."

Caywood wrote it down dutifully.

"Did Quentin Stanley behave as he usually did on the last day he worked here?"

"He left early. He walked off and left me with a great bundle to get to the dustbin. Looked at that big gold watch of his, put it back in his pocket, and just left."

"As if he had an appointment to keep?"

"Yes, sir."

"Did he say where he was going?"

"Not to me, he didn't. Quentin never spoke to me."

"Did he seem happy or worried or frightened, for that matter?" Caywood pressed.

"No, just the same. Same old Quentin," the maid said.

Mrs. Sare looked at the inspector, who nodded. "You may go now, Kitty," she said.

"Thank you, Mrs. Sare."

"When does your husband get home, Mrs. Sare? I want to ask him a few questions as well."

"Usually late, Inspector. About seven or seven-thirty, but he knows nothing."

"I'll come after dinner tonight and try to get through as quickly as possible." Caywood put his notebook back in his pocket. "By the way, Mrs. Sare, how long have you and Mr. Sare lived in Cheamley?"

"Not very long. We're outsiders. We've been here only eighteen years, but we'd be strangers had we lived here for a hundred years. They just are difficult people," she said matter-of-factly.

"A bit standoffish, aren't they?" Caywood smiled. "Thank you very much, Mrs. Sare. I'll see you again tonight."

She led him to the door and let him out into the cold wind. He tightened his muffler, and when there was no response to his knock at the Thompsons', Caywood crossed the road and headed toward the church hall. He saw P.C. Dexter leaving Hazel Weller's and signaled him.

"The Thompsons are never home at this hour. I'll try to question them tonight when I get back to Cheamley. If you will tackle Mr. Kenneth Keith, I'll get the next one on the list, Miss Fields."

"Right," said Dexter, talkative as ever.

"Did you get to the others up the road?"

"Yes, the newslady and Mrs. Gill and Miss Weller. No change in their stories."

"Then that will leave only three or four more."

"Right."

"Right," agreed Peter Caywood.

Amanda Fields proved to be the only other intriguing woman in a village of dullards. Perhaps it was because he'd yet to tackle the men that Cheamley seemed to be a misplaced planet of Amazons.

Once admitted to Miss Fields's cottage, he was overwhelmed by heavy perfume that contrasted with an unending collection of glass figurines, crystal animals, and painted leprechauns that crowded the tables and shelves of her crowded lounge. The front window had gauzy curtains that let light in. Thereafter it was captured by one piece of crystal, bounced to another figure of glass, until the entire room intensified and reflected whatever light Cheamley was allotted that day.

Even after she spoke, Caywood could not decide whether Miss Fields belonged to the crystal or heavy perfume. He wondered how the ladies of Cheamley felt about Amanda Fields. Once past the glitter of glass, he saw what a beauty she was, how desirable she was. He guessed how the men of the village felt. She wore lipstick a bit too crimson and a purple blouse that tugged a bit too taut across her formidable breasts.

"Did you know Quentin Stanley?"

"Course, who didn't?"

"Did you see him this past Wednesday, by any chance?"

"Crossing the road, didn't I?"

"What time?"

"What time? A little past two it was, wasn't it?"

Caywood couldn't decide who was questioning whom. Whenever he asked a question, she responded with one. Whenever she responded, she moistened her full lips with a darting tongue that made them a deeper red.

Caywood caught his breath and got his thoughts back to business. "In which direction was he going?"

"Was he going where?"

"That's what I want to know," he pushed and wished only briefly that he'd left this one to Dexter. He avoided looking at her blouse. "In which direction?"

"I dunno. The church, I think," she said.

He waited for a question and realised it was his turn. "Did Quentin Stanley work for you?"

"Work for me?"

He expected that. "Did he work for you, house cleaning, that sort of thing?"

"Me? I'm not one of the royals."

Caywood had not guessed that.

"No, he didn't work for me. How could I afford a dustman?"

"What sort of work do you do?"

"I'm a barmaid in Rumsden."

"Oh really. Where do you work?"

"At the Victoria Arms."

Caywood made a mental note not to take Eliza there. "What time did you get home last Wednesday?"

"Didn't *get* home. *Was* home. Day off."

"Did anyone see you?"

"See me? No, I never went out. Saw the old man going toward the woods."

"Do you live here alone?" Caywood wrote steadily in his leather book.

"Yes, I do. My girl friend Rita up and married six months ago, so I've had to go it alone."

"Did you like Quentin Stanley?"

"I dunno, do I? Never spoke to him in my whole life."

"Did you see anything unusual Wednesday?"

She twisted her face, furrowed her brow, and Caywood waited patiently while she squeezed her brain.

"No," she said.

"Well, thank you very much, Miss Fields. If you think of anything that might help us solve this case, please do let me know. By the way, you have a beautiful collection of glass."

"Not mine. It's Rita's. I do wish she'd come get it out of the way."

That answered that, Caywood thought as he put his cap back on. It was snowing now. He decided it was time for tea. He cut across the road and then the green, passed the Clemsons', and entered the tea shop that was between the chemist's and the butcher.

The sign said CHEAMLEY TEA SHOPPE and beneath it in small gilt letters, MISSES FLORENCE AND LYDIA KNIGHT, PROPS. He smelled fresh bread as he entered.

How nice, Caywood thought. Once he'd looked around the room, again he thought, How nice. The place was airy, with a glow of pink and old lavender, just the place for dear old ladies. Suddenly he felt quite out of place, the intruder that he actually was. The tables had pink covers of some easily cleansed plastic material. What saved this practical intrusion were delicate lace-hemmed place mats. Caywood was a bull in this china shop and was immediately a man on the defensive rather than the inspector in charge. He picked up the handwritten menu carefully and put it down as quickly. All finger sandwiches and broth.

The room was beginning to fill with some of the villagers that Caywood had already met. They seemed to sniff as they passed him on their way to the five other tables in the room. There were two window seats that remained vacant.

"Good morning, sir. What would you like this morning?" She was a white-haired, blue-eyed sprite of a woman, who walked rapidly between the tables, serving, clearing dishes, cleaning. Caywood had watched her, fascinated by her agility and balancing power.

"Oh, good morning. You surprised me."

"I'm that sorry I startled you, sir," she replied.

"Miss Knight?"

"Yes, I'm Florence."

"Miss Knight, I'm Inspector Caywood. I need to talk to you and your sister about Quentin Stanley."

"Oh my," she fluttered.

"Not to worry, Miss Knight. I'll wait until you are less rushed. Actually I am famished, so I'll have coffee, white, please."

"Anything else?"

He pulled up the menu again. "And some sticky gingerbread, please. I haven't had any in quite a long time."

"Yes, right away, sir."

Caywood noticed that she whispered something into the ear of the other white-haired lady, who was pouring coffee at a serving stand in the rear of the shop. She dropped a cup that crashed into the hardwood floor. Conversation ceased for a second, and then the noise built up again.

When Miss Florence Knight returned, she placed coffee before him. "Sorry, no more gingerbread, so I've brought some scones. Will that be all right?"

"Yes, certainly. They look delicious." He dawdled over two cups of coffee and five scones, all thickly buttered. Soon enough the tea shop was empty, and all he heard was the din of clattering cups and the ring of the cash register as they straightened up for the morning. Caywood stood up as the two ladies came to his table.

"Please sit down, Inspector. This is my sister, Lydia. Here, I've brought us some tea. We could all do with a wee rest," Florence Knight tittered.

Caywood took the tray and smiled at Lydia. They looked like twins, even in their antiquity.

Lydia Knight poured thick yellow cream into the pink-flowered cups. The tea she poured must have been a special blend. It smelled different from what they had been pouring since he'd been there.

She noticed Caywood casually sniffing the air. "Ceylon," she said sheepishly.

"Oh yes." He looked pleased as he took the cup.

"Now, about Quentin," Florence said. "What is it you want to know?"

"Did you know him well?" Caywood asked.

"He never came in for tea, if that's what you mean," Lydia said.

"No, not exactly. Did he work for you? Did he do any cleaning?"

"On rare occasions," Florence answered as her sister sipped her tea. "We're well organised."

"Did you see him this Wednesday past?"

Lydia looked at Florence. They shook their heads in unison. Caywood let a smile escape him. "Do you remember anything unusual happening on Wednesday?"

"No, not that I recall," Florence replied. Lydia agreed.

"Where were you ladies on Wednesday night?" Caywood asked.

"At choir practice, of course."

"And what time did you leave?"

"I don't recall exactly. We left with Caroline Clemson, I think," Florence said.

"Yes, I believe we did," Lydia said.

"Thank you, ladies, for the information and a lovely tea." He walked back to the cash register and left some money there. The ladies Knight beamed as he walked out of the shop.

When Caywood returned to the incident centre in the church hall, he ignored the ladies who were fluttering around looking like so many ruffled hens.

"Where are we to go?" he heard one of them say in a loud stage whisper.

"We have to plan the jumble," another one answered, keeping up the din. "Police!" she spat out.

Caywood never missed a step. He dared not. Just as he reached the alcove he'd taken for his office, he saw Caroline Clemson smiling sympathetically. It was worth running the gauntlet. Poor Mrs. Clemson, he thought, caught in the jumble sale. He sat down, tossed his cap on the desk, and let out a long, deep sigh. On top of the box was a long brown envelope that he tackled at once.

There was a translation of the German birth certificate of James Stanley. The male child was born in Frankfurt on June 8, 1943. Older than me, Caywood thought, but is it correct? The mother was listed as Elsa Koch and the father was Quentin Stanley. Caywood let out another great sigh. With the translation was an enlargement of the boy's photograph. He looked bright, but poorly dressed. Caywood wondered what had happened to Elsa Koch.

"Good afternoon, Chief Inspector."

Caywood looked up to see Harry Kirk wearing a Harris tweed cap identical to his own. He was annoyed but said, "You look fit, Harry. How do you feel? You didn't take much time off."

"The doctor said it was psychosomatic because of my trouble with Angela."

"A psychosomatic chill?" Caywood raised his eyebrows in amazement.

"Told me to keep my head covered."

Caywood tried not to smile. "Look here, Harry. I've got the first lead, maybe." He motioned to Kirk to sit down. "This birth certificate lists Stanley as the father of a child who as of now has more than reached his majority."

"The boy in the picture?"

"The older one, I believe," Caywood said. "The smaller boy was Stanley's brother who died."

"I would guess this boy"—he gave Kirk the photo—"is James Stanley."

"I know the next step."

"Yes, find James Stanley, and I think I know where to begin." He looked up at Kirk again. "Are you certain you can work today?"

"Yes, sir."

"Well, P.C. Dexter is out getting the rest of the villagers' statements. I want you to give Quentin Stanley's cottage and premises another going-over. You find what I have missed. Now I'm going to find a lady named Clemson in that crowd of hens and have a long chat. So let's get this business closed." Caywood straightened his brown silk necktie. "Nice cap," he said to Kirk as he left the room.

"Oh thank you, Inspector."

Caywood trod gingerly through the ladies' jumble sale preparation committee and reached Caroline Clemson, who sat on the far side of the room.

"Inspector." She beamed. "I admire your courage."

"This is one of the days I admire it as well, Mrs. Clemson. I need your help. Do you mind coming to my office here and looking at something for me?"

"Be happy to." She rose from the chair and took Caywood's arm.

They reached his alcove, where he put the photo before her. "Do you know this child?"

"No, Inspector." She looked at it closely. "No, I don't know who this child is. He never lived in Cheamley."

"Oh." Caywood's disappointment was all over his face. "To the best of my knowledge it's Quentin Stanley's son."

"Couldn't be," Mrs. Clemson protested. "Quentin never married, Inspector."

Caywood smiled. "It's his child by some German fräulein."

"Doesn't look like Quentin. I don't think it's his child. Funny . . ." She looked at the picture again. Caywood thought she was lost in memory.

"Yes?"

She fluttered a bit. "Colin stood just that way when he was that age. Oh well, Inspector, sorry I couldn't help."

Caywood escorted Mrs. Clemson back to her place in the centre hall before exposing himself again to Cheamley's main street and to Stanley's cottage. He joined Kirk in one last search before they returned to the church hall for the inquest.

The inquiry into the death of one Quentin Stanley was as novel to Cheamley as had been the death itself. Vicar Morgan provided the site in one of the church hall rooms that once had served as a nursery. Now all the babies had outgrown it. Derek and Rose Adams, who had successively used one of the old cribs, sat on the front row of chairs between their parents. The old cribs, now dust-covered and cobwebbed, were pushed into the rear of the room. Faded pictures of the Virgin Mary and Jesus gathered dust on the wall behind six rows of folding chairs that faced a raised platform in the front.

Behind a black table on the platform sat Mr. Marsdon, the district coroner. He was a white, soapy-faced, emaciated man with an uneven, high-pitched voice. In spite of the fact that he looked and sounded like a discarded cat with less than one life to live, Mr. Marsdon handled the proceedings with impressive expertise. In the front row were P.C. Dexter and Vicar Morgan, next to the Adamses. One chair was vacant and being held for the police examiner. Caywood and Kirk tucked their long legs under the miserable chairs and awaited their turn to answer. Mr. Marsdon was as annoyed with Dr. Wick's tardiness as the rest of the villagers who crowded in for the event. Except for Mrs. Clemson, the entire jumble sale committee of ladies came and waited for gory details. They were disappointed. Dr. Wick, who arrived ten minutes late, stated that Quentin Stanley had died of a massive cerebral hemorrhage caused by trauma—a blunt instrument, to be precise.

"What was the time of death?" the coroner asked.

"Between 10:30 P.M. and midnight. Eleven o'clock is my best estimate," Wick said. "Wednesday night."

"Is that the best time estimate, Doctor?" Mr. Marsdon asked.

"It was quite cold. The body was frozen," Wick stated.

Caywood smiled as the police surgeon was prodded by the coroner.

"Where did the death occur?" Marsdon asked.

"In the graveyard of St. Mary's Church here in Cheamley. The wounds were severe enough that the man probably dropped on the spot."

"What is your conclusion?" the coroner prodded Wick once more.

"Mr. Quentin Stanley was murdered on Wednesday night, November 17, at 11 P.M."

Mr. Marsdon thanked Dr. Wick and asked Detective Chief Inspector Caywood whether they had found the instrument. When Caywood answered in the negative, Mr. Marsdon adjourned the inquest, satisfied at least that the body had been identified and that the deceased had been murdered.

It was obvious that the disappointment of the church's ladies was turning into anger. They had no return on what they had given up to the police. They twitted and grumbled as they filed out of the room. Rose Adams was carried out in her father's arms. She was crying, and Caywood felt sorry for the poor child.

CHAPTER 6

Man-Child

Quentin Stanley's funeral was a quiet, poorly attended event that seemed to Caywood to be squeezed between the jumble sale preparation and an early choir practice for the children. Mrs. Clemson attended; and when he saw the empty church, Caywood gathered his men to fill the empty pews and serve as pallbearers as well. The vicar's housekeeper was there, as was Hazel Weller in her wheelchair.

Vicar Morgan went through the service slowly, as if to emphasize that there was some worth to Quentin Stanley's life in this final tribute to him.

The snowstorm stopped long enough for them to bury Stanley in a grave not too far from where his body had been found. As they lowered the coffin, Caywood noticed the Adams children clinging to their mother. When it was over, he got his constables back to work.

"I hope I never have to do that again," P.C. Dexter whispered.

"We'll all do what's called for," Caywood advised him. "The least we can do for a victim, much less another human being. Sorry you feel put upon," he said softly, with an authority not lost on the complainer.

When Caywood stepped from the cemetery into the church hall, he found Wilson Wick's report, which seemed to be the final flower on Quentin Stanley's grave. Caywood opened the folder and was happy to find that good old Wick had a memo clipped to the official report. It read:

Dear Peter,

As I said at the inquest, the man died as a result of a blow to the head that caused a skull fracture that produced a brain hemorrhage.

Best ever,
Wick

Following the note were thirty pages of single-spaced typewritten gore. Caywood flipped through it and scanned descriptions of heart, lungs, liver, and various other anatomical odds and ends.

"Good old Wick," Caywood murmured. He locked the report in his briefcase and made his way out of the hall to the trilling of children's voices. He headed down the road to The Angels in Green. Halfway there he saw Kirk and his damnable new cap locking the door of the Stanley cottage.

"Harry," he shouted.

They joined forces for a brief respite at The Angels, as the natives referred to the pub. There were two men at one end of the polished bar finishing a pint together with light yellow cheese and dark brown bread. There was a middle-aged woman sitting at the table nursing a glass of wine. A young couple, glued to each other's eyes and hand in hand, let their soup and coffee grow cold. Caywood looked around, not recognising anyone except Nigel Martin, the publican.

"I had a great tea this morning with the Knight ladies. Filled me up so much that I forgot about lunch."

"I'm famished," Kirk confessed. "I hope the cat stays out of my way."

Caywood smiled as he saw the fire roaring and the cat in the seat next to it. She rose, stretched, arching her back up high, padding her front paws well out, then up her back went again. Just as suddenly she lay down, circled herself, and went to sleep. When Kirk sat next to her, her top hind leg thrust hard into his right thigh.

"Shall we call her Angela or Eliza?" Caywood mused.

"Neither," Kirk replied. "Cat serves a purpose."

Caywood went to the counter and inspected the hot side of the food bar. "Shepherd pies, two pints, please," he ordered.

As they ate, Kirk pulled out an envelope of odds and ends he'd found at Stanley's.

"What the devil are these?" Caywood asked as he spread some stubs out before them.

"Look like bus stubs. I found them stuck in various places, one in a coat pocket, another under a paper in a drawer. I think they're stubs he simply put in his pocket or on his nightstand rather than tossing them away on the ground."

"They're pretty worn. Can you make them out?"

"Yes. Here." Kirk handed Caywood a magnifying glass.

"Regular Sherlock Holmes, aren't you? You need to get another kind of hat."

Kirk smiled a rather small, triumphant smile. "This will do. Thank you, sir."

"The ticket is for Watering, as I make it out. Where the devil is that?"

"Beyond Collier and Rossmore. It's about fifty miles from here. It would be an all-day trip on one of these old buses."

"Ring up Watering CID and check for motor registration or any sign of James Stanley."

"Do you think he owns a motorcar?" Kirk asked.

"One never knows, but if in fact he does, we'll have a great record from which to work."

"Right." Kirk realised his stupidity.

"Just because Quentin was a poor wretch doesn't mean his son will be the same. If you can't find a license, then I'll drive over there and come back to talk to the Sares. I want you to finish up all the questioning. Take Dexter with you. He was supposed to review everything tomorrow, unless, of course, there are more problems."

The cat jabbed a paw into Kirk's thigh.

"Cat's getting a bit testy, Inspector."

"Dangle a piece of beef in front of her."

When he did, she came straight up like a shark and swallowed it whole.

"Did you see that? Never even opened an eye."

"Years of practice. Are you ready?" Caywood asked.

"Right with you." Kirk patted the cat, followed Caywood out of The Angels in Green, and left the inspector at his car. Kirk pulled his new cap down.

Caywood missed the gesture as he cleared the windscreen of ice and snow. By four-thirty he was in Watering CID being helped by a duty sergeant who seemed mildly interested in the problem. He was a tall, black-haired man wearing silver-wire-rimmed glasses. Sergeant Afstron looked more like an accountant than a policeman. He checked his records, made some phone calls, and set Chief Inspector Caywood up to a steaming cup of dark brown tea while he waited.

"Some good luck, Chief Inspector. I have three James Stanleys in this district."

"How old? Mine would be in his late thirties or early forties, I think. Here's a photo."

Sergeant Afstron flipped through his cards. "I think this is the fellow. The others are too young. But you are in trouble if this fellow is a witness."

Caywood put his cup down on the desk and took the records. Afstron went on, "This Stanley is at St. Agnes Hospital. It's a mental place."

"Let's have the directions, and many thanks." Caywood drained the last bit of tea and, once in his car, spread out a street map on the seat beside him.

Watering was nearly as large as Rumsden, with narrow stone streets that followed no pattern, not even the map. It was getting quite dark by the time he reached the gates of St. Agnes Hospital. He left the car in a park about one square away and made his way on cobbled walks to the entrance. The foyer was small, overflowing with Victorian bric-a-brac and a single statue of whom Caywood presumed to be St. Agnes. It was a dark, oppressive, almost forbidding place. There was a glassed-in area with an office behind. Caywood tapped. He tapped it a third time before a sister appeared.

"Sister," Caywood spoke through a small circular opening in the glass, "I am Detective Chief Inspector Peter Caywood." He displayed his identification close enough for her to read. "I'm looking for a James Stanley. Watering CID says he is here."

"Yes, Inspector, James Stanley has been here since childhood, long before I came."

He heard her unlocking a great black door that was to his left.

"I am Sister Elizabeth." She led him through another hall into a small windowless office. "Please sit down." She pointed to one of two straight chairs.

She went into an alcove that Caywood missed seeing at first. When she returned, she placed a yellowing folder on the desk between them and switched on the green gooseneck lamp to her left.

"Here is all the information that we have. You can see that James came as a small child, nearly an infant."

"Does the record report who brought the child here and why?"

She turned the folder in Caywood's direction. "Here, see for yourself, Inspector."

Caywood thumbed through the pages as the nun continued to talk.

"James is mentally retarded. He was born in Germany toward the end of or after the war. His father, Quentin Stanley, brought him here. Apparently the mother died in Germany."

"How did he get a baby out of Germany at the end of the war?" Caywood wondered out loud.

"Volumes of red tape, boxes of paperwork, considerable heartbreak as well, I'm sure."

"Did Quentin visit the child?"

"Every week. Nearly every Sunday and sometimes Thursdays if he couldn't come on Sundays. And," she added, "he paid for James's upkeep."

"Always?"

"What he could at first, according to the record. More later."

"And recently?"

"James has had to have more care. Quentin somehow managed a good surgeon and hospital."

"When was this?" Caywood pressed the issue.

"About two years ago."

"May I see James, Sister? I'm afraid I have bad news for him. Quentin was murdered."

"Yes, I read of his death and contacted our bishop."

"Do you think he will understand?"

"Perhaps. He is older than anyone else here, but a child in his mind, you see. We'll try together."

"Yes," Caywood agreed.

They walked up worn stairs to the fourth floor. The silence of the place was surprising.

"James's room is at the end of the hall." She knocked and opened the door. "James, look who's here. A friend of your father's to talk to you."

Above the single bed was a crucifix, on the bedside table a photo of Quentin Stanley and a lamp. The room was nearly bare otherwise. There was a desk and chair. On the desk were some ragged children's books. Caywood looked from the books to the middle-aged man who sat on the bed. He was not at all prepared for what he saw, an old man who looked older than either him or Quentin. His face was childlike, and his speech the same. His clothes were simple and clean.

"James, do you remember your father?"

James smiled.

"The man who comes to see you every week is your father," Sister Elizabeth said.

The man continued to smile, but it was obvious to Caywood that he did not comprehend.

"I'm sorry to tell you, James, that your father has died."

"Yes," the man on the bed said. "Too bad."

"Yes, too bad, James," Caywood said. "He won't be coming to visit you anymore."

"Too bad, too bad," he said again.

"Well, I must be going, James." Caywood reached over and patted him on the shoulder.

"Go to bed now, James," the nun said. She walked ahead of Caywood to the stairs.

"What will happen to him now?"

"We'll take care of him. Don't worry, Inspector."

It was seven-thirty when he reached the car park. Caywood sat for a while, trying to let it all register. He reached for the silver and black case. There were two cigarettes left. He lit one and let the motor turn over and over in the cold until it finally caught.

What a burden, he thought, one that Quentin carried all his life. What had happened two years ago? Blackmail, it had to have been blackmail. He drove steadily toward Cheamley, sifting through his mind the people he'd questioned. He kept driving, ignoring the signposts. Absentmindedly he reached for his last cigarette. Suddenly he realised he was on the outskirts of Rumsden. Too tired to turn back to Cheamley, he drove to Eliza's.

He rang up Kirk from her flat.

"I'm here at Miss Crisp's," he informed him, and then in a loud voice, "I'm terribly tired and hope she will feed me. Later I'll be at my flat." He listened for a minute. "Yes, that's all right, but, Harry, the trip to Watering paid off." He paused. "Yes, it was Stanley's son, quite an old man, at least he looks it. Now listen, Harry, you need to talk to Desmond Sare tonight if you can. Keep the business about James Stanley under your new cap." He chuckled. "Yes, do that, there's a good fellow." He hung up the receiver.

"Aren't you going to take pity and feed me?" he smiled his best.

"Fat chance." Eliza adjusted the earring on her left earlobe.

"Oh come on, old girl. It's been a rough day."

"And what do you think I've been doing? Sitting by hearth and fire? I was not. We inventoried all the Christmas stock for the third time and came up short again. Someone is stealing me blind. A lot of help the police are."

"Eliza, why not just be CEO and keep your hands out of the store?"

"Because, my dear Peter, there will not be a board to be CEO of unless someone minds the store, so to speak."

"Will you feed me, my love?"

He did look tired, she decided. "Oh very well." She went into the kitchen with Caywood close behind.

"Do I have any choice?" he asked.

"Eggs, eggs, or eggs." She put a bowl of them on the table with one hand and fetched a skillet with the other. She dumped three eggs and one tablespoon of water in a bowl and beat them with a vengeance.

"You're supposed to be beating the eggs, not killing them."

"Believe me, they're already dead."

"Best they are."

Her kitchen was as white and shining as a laboratory. Even the skillet was white. She was as efficient as her kitchen looked. Within ten minutes she placed before him an omelet, toast, marmalade, and a cup of dark tea.

"Aren't you eating?" he asked.

"No. Clive is picking me up for dinner."

"I cannot believe this, Eliza. Why are you going out with that ass?" Caywood put down his knife and fork in disgust.

"Because he asked me, which is considerably better than any recent offer from you, I must say."

"Lizzie, I've had an unbelievably bad day. Please be just a little kind." He reached over and took her hand. She sensed his desperation.

"What happened?" she asked softly.

"Some chaps are always the refuse of society through no fault of their own. I tracked down Quentin Stanley's child. Only he's not a child. He's a retarded old man who sits in a spartan room on the fourth floor of a mental institution. He's been there for maybe thirty years. I had to tell him that the only person in this world who cared for him is dead. It breaks my heart, Eliza."

She reached over and kissed him. "You're my tough policeman, Caywood. Don't let them get to you."

The telephone rang. She went to answer while he dawdled over the eggs.

"Who was that?" he asked.

"Clive."

"Oh?"

"I told him I had a headache."

Caywood smiled. "Come on, dear Lizzie, I'll take you out for a drink."

"The devil with you, Peter. You'd lead me down the path again with all your sad talk. Food and tender loving care, that's what you wanted. I warn you, it will never happen again."

Five minutes later they were in his car, a sensible coat draped around Eliza's shoulders and a borrowed pack of Benson and Hedges for him. From time to time he glanced at her and knew how lucky he was to have this intelligent, beautiful woman beside him.

"What are the stealing glances about? Keep your eyes on the road."

"Just admiring you."

"Don't trifle with my affections. You're in love with my cooking."

He laughed. "Well, actually, that's true. But I was thinking about the green-and-blue necktie."

"That blasted thing!" She laughed with him, an out-of-character girlish giggle. "You know, we've never stocked that wretched line again."

He became silent, lost in his thoughts about when they'd met. How he had bought a second-rate striped silk tie and brought it back to Crisp's, demanded to see the buyer, who turned out to be Eliza, the store owner. She soothed his ruffled feathers, exchanged it for a brown silk one, and gave him tea.

Now she read his mind. "Not only did you get a new, and I might add a better one, but a cup of tea in the bargain, and I've had you on my hands ever since."

He roared.

"Look out, Peter. You nearly ran that old lady down. For heaven's sake, do be careful. And where the devil are we going?"

"Just ahead." He pulled the car over and got the last place in the car park.

She looked around for signs of a restaurant or, heaven forbid, a pub. "Please tell me it's not Chinese."

"It's not. Look to your left. It's Italian."

"I can hardly wait."

"A little Chianti, my dear, and you'll think you're in heaven."

She ordered Sauternes instead with a small green salad, to be followed by coffee, white.

"You'll insult these people with such an order," Caywood protested.

"I'm sure you'll eat enough for both of us in spite of the omelet."

She was correct, of course. He ate pasta loaded with sauce, wiped it up with garlic bread, and drowned it with Chianti. Eliza kept her window open all the way home. She heard the telephone ringing as they walked in.

"For you." She handed him the phone.

"Yes, Harry. No, you didn't wake me up." Caywood put his hand over the mouthpiece. "Cheeky bastard," he said to Eliza. "I'll come right now."

"What's happened?" she asked.

"Another one of those dull villagers has been done in." He kissed her good night.

CHAPTER 7

Down to the Sea

Caywood bypassed the activity at the bridge and went directly to the church hall, where Kirk was waiting.

"It's pretty ghastly," Kirk warned him.

"Who is it?"

"We think it's Hazel Weller, but we're not at all certain."

"Police surgeon here yet?"

"No, but he's on his way. I expect he'll be there." Kirk led the way down the road to the north bridge that spanned the Rumsden River. The shops were dark, as was The Angels. Kirk flashed his torch ahead of them down the slippery slope that led to the river.

"How do you s'pose a lady in a wheelchair made her way down here?" Caywood wondered.

Kirk skirted the area with his torch, outlining the local geography like a rapidly turning kaleidoscope. The river was frozen, unusual for November, yet the river didn't have a calendar. Kirk flooded his light onto a particular bit of the landscape, a dinghy frozen in the river. In the boat was the body of a woman. She lay facedown, arms outstretched, head hanging over into the ice that her face had smashed. Now her head appeared to be trapped in ice that had refrozen around her.

"Get some more lights down here before you trample all the evidence into the ice," Caywood commanded. "What's the matter with you?"

The photographer tramped over the snow-covered bank, down to the ice-crested shoreline, and flashed his camera in every and all blinding directions. Caywood heard his boots crunch through the icy water. Wilson Wick stood beside Caywood.

"I thought this was a quiet little village, Inspector."

"As quiet as this frozen river, Dr. Wick, but the water below is something else."

"Haven't you enough pictures?" Wick shouted to the photographer. "It's damned cold out here. I want to get through and get home to my warm bed. Hurry up, man. You aren't training for the cinema."

"Right, sir. I'm out of your way this instant." There was a mocking tone to his voice.

"Go ahead, Wick. Don't let that young pup bother you."

"Thank you, Inspector. I am forever in your debt."

Caywood told the photographer to come up on the bank. "Don't go away," Caywood told him. "What's your name?"

"Dawson, sir."

"Good man, Dawson. Now, when the police surgeon is ready, he'll need your help. By the way, how long have you been with us at Rumsden?"

"Brand new, sir. Three weeks."

"Oh, Dr. Wick is signaling for you. You can leave your camera with Sergeant Kirk. He'll bring it down when you're ready."

The new boy slid down to the dinghy.

"I hope Wick doesn't rub too much sparkle off our photographer," Caywood said.

He saw Wick climb into the boat and try to lift up the victim. "Here," he called to the photographer, "ease your way out to the woman's head and see if you can free it from the ice."

"I find it hard to believe that a physician has so little compassion. New boy will freeze his—"

"Derriere off," Caywood interrupted Kirk. They both heard the boy groan as he waded through the freezing water, his thighs crushing the crusty upper layer of ice. Quickly he freed the woman's head from the ice.

"Get out of the water fast, Dawson," Caywood shouted at him as he and Kirk eased down the bank. Caywood extended his left hand out as far as he could and pulled Dawson up. The dinghy rocked with Dawson's effort to get out of the water, causing Dr. Wick to lose his balance. Cursing, he fell forward on the corpse. Kirk went to the surgeon's rescue, while poor Dawson, too cold and numb to complain, practically crawled up the bank.

"Let's pull the dinghy up and rope off the area. Wick, get out of there," Caywood ordered. "Kirk and I are going to pull her up." There was no argument. By the time they were ready, two constables had set up battery lights. Caywood helped Wick turn the corpse over.

"The murderer did quite a job," Wick said.

"When do you think she died?"

"Hard to say. She's frozen stiff, and I'm not being flippant, believe me." Wick looked up. "We need that photographer again."

"You nearly killed him. What a shameful thing to do to a new man," Caywood muttered through his chattering teeth. He pushed his jacket collar up and hunched his neck down to meet it.

The wind buffeted the floodlights, giving the whole scene of frozen river, dinghy, snowbound bank, an eerie, surrealistic quality.

"Go on up, Inspector. No point in all of us getting pneumonia."

"I think I'd better stay until this young fellow finishes his photos." Caywood motioned toward the victim's face.

She had been beaten nearly beyond recognition. Globs of clotted blood were frozen to her face. Her left eye lay in a collapsed state in its orbit like a dead fish's eye. The nose was flattened around her face. The swollen blue lips were parted in final, futile protest. Her hands were gloved in blood. Her clothes were saturated in it and glazed over with ice.

Dawson had acquired some high rubber boots and a thick yellow sweater that hung on him like a choir boy. Caywood thought if the new boy got through this night he would have won considerable respect. He stood steady and took an extraordinary number of photos.

"I say, Dawson, is your finger frozen to the shutter?" The fellow looked grateful. "Dawson, tell Kirk to ask the vicar if you can have some hot tea or something."

The ambulance arrived and the poor soul's body was carried away.

"All right. Start circling in," Caywood ordered. "Kirk, go up on the bridge. See what you can find and then go over the dinghy in place, anything, everything."

Kirk's red beard was now frosted with blowing snow. He signaled Dawson to accompany him on the bridge for more photos.

"I've already been, Sergeant."

"The body's been removed. Come take some more."

Dawson waddled in his ill-fitting boots up to the bridge and, in order to satisfy all, photographed from the opposite side of the bank as well.

Caywood knew their chances of finding evidence in the wind, snow, and ice were small, but his crew persisted in their efforts for three more hours. He drove slowly back to his flat in Rumsden, fighting off sleep, lighting one cigarette after another, his car window open. It was nearly 4 A.M. when Caywood fell onto his bed. He didn't bother to undress, just fell into bed and slept.

CHAPTER 8

Bloody Places

Caywood slept two hours, and when he returned to Cheamley it was still quite early in the morning. Kirk had the constables organised as well as any sleep-bereft crew could be.

"I have them out questioning everyone all over again. They've completed the list except for the Sares and one or two others."

"Have you found anything at all?"

"Well . . . we confirmed it was Hazel Weller. I've been to her cottage and plan to go through it again."

"Let's do this, Harry. We'll take these last people together, and I've never talked to the Thompsons. We can go over Weller's cottage later."

"What do you think?" Kirk asked.

"If we think Stanley was a blackmailer, then the logical sequence is that she tried to take over his victim and became one herself. She obviously made someone very angry," Caywood said. "You told your men that there ought to be some bloody clothes somewhere in this village this morning?"

"Yes, Inspector, they know to look for bloodied clothes and any possible weapon. We are searching every cottage. There was no blood at Weller's."

"Impossible. We'll give it another overhaul."

They went first to the Sares', where they arrived at 8 A.M. Mrs. Sare was fresh and wide awake when she opened the door. She led them into the library and offered them coffee while they waited for Desmond Sare to finish dressing.

The room was comfortable. In addition to a great walnut desk that dominated the room, there were two small sofas covered in brown tweed facing each other in front of an elegantly tiled hearth and fireplace. On the left wall was a large television surrounded by bookshelves. The shelves extended around the room.

"Interesting collection," Caywood commented. "Shakespeare, some modern plays, boys' books, art history."

Kirk concentrated on his coffee.

"He has quite a collection of travel books." Caywood continued his tour of the Sares' books when a middle-aged man about Caywood's height came into the room.

"Desmond Sare, Chief Inspector." He extended a firm hand. Caywood smelled a refreshing cologne on the fellow, who was a little less than six feet tall and whose light brown hair was growing thin on top. He had penetrating brown eyes that offset a broad smile and wore a small red carnation in his buttonhole.

"This is Sergeant Kirk, Mr. Sare."

Sare motioned for them to sit down as he pulled a straight chair up close to the fireplace.

"This is an early call," he said. His voice was somewhat high-pitched and out of character for this muscular man. His deep-set brown eyes darted quickly from Caywood to Kirk. His clothes were well cut, and Caywood assessed them to be expensive.

"We're terribly sorry to interrupt you this morning. Perhaps you've heard that Hazel Weller was murdered last night. So we do need your help."

"Good Lord," Sare said softly. "Old Hazel? Why on earth?" He seemed to be talking to himself.

"Did you know either Miss Weller or Mr. Quentin Stanley?" Caywood asked.

"Oh, I knew them when I saw them," Sare said. "I saw them on rare occasions in the village. As you know, Stanley worked for us, but I didn't know them other than to say 'good morning' and the like."

Sare took a cigarette from the gold case in his inside jacket pocket. He offered one to the policemen. Caywood took one and immediately appreciated the aroma of a special blend.

"Thank you." Caywood took a long drag as soon as it was lit.

"When did you last see Miss Weller?" Kirk let Caywood enjoy his smoke.

"I really don't know. It may have been weeks ago or it may have been months ago. As far as having any personal conversation, I can tell you for a fact that I never said more than three words to the woman."

"And Quentin Stanley?" Caywood asked.

"Oh, at least three, maybe four weeks ago, although he was here every week."

"What day did he usually come?" Kirk asked.

"You'll have to ask my wife. I don't know." He laughed. "That's her department."

"She said Stanley was here last Wednesday, the day he was murdered."

"I didn't see him, Inspector. I leave early and return late."

"Where do you work, Mr. Sare?"

"I have my own business. We manufacture furniture, mainly."

"In Rumsden?"

"Yes, and we have stores in Watering and Rossmore and one in Harton."

"Do you visit all of the plants?" Caywood asked.

"In rotation, one week here, the next there."

"When were you in Watering?"

"Three weeks ago, as I recall."

"Where were you Wednesday past?"

"At work, in Rumsden."

"And when did you arrive home?"

"I don't know, Inspector. Probably around eight. My wife usually knows where I am."

"She says you were here."

"Well, that's good to know," he said laughingly.

"Did you like Quentin Stanley?" Kirk asked.

"I didn't know either Stanley or Hazel Weller well enough to like or dislike them. And that's the truth."

"Very well, Mr. Sare. We won't keep you any longer, but we will stay a bit longer to talk to Mrs. Sare and the children."

Sare squashed his cigarette in a blue marbleized ashtray. "Stay here, gentlemen, I'll ask Mrs. Sare and the children to come in."

"Don't disturb Mrs. Sare. Sergeant Kirk can talk to her in the kitchen and perhaps I can talk to the children here. What are their names?"

"Knox and Hannah," Sare said and left the room with Kirk following. Caywood remembered the names as soon as he heard them.

The children were somewhat shy. Caywood expected a dominant father figure like Desmond Sare had much to do with that.

Knox was the older, a tall, slim, handsome boy who looked more like his mother. He wore an old-fashioned gold watch chain, far too ornate for such a young boy. His knee stockings were neat and his shoes highly polished. Hannah was stocky, a sturdy girl in a pink dress. Her face was pretty. She would mature into a lovely woman.

"I'm Detective Chief Inspector Caywood," he introduced himself to the Sare children.

Knox shook hands, a firm handshake for a young boy. "I'm Knox. This is my sister, Hannah."

"I s'pose your mother told you why I'm here. Hazel Weller and Quentin Stanley are dead. Do you know of any reason why someone would want to kill them?"

"No," Hannah said nervously. She twisted a long blond curl by her right ear.

"Sit down, Hannah. Please don't be frightened." Her face was quivering. "Now, Hannah, it's all right," Caywood said softly.

"Don't be afraid, Hannah," her brother urged her to be calm.

"Where were you last night and last Wednesday night?"

"We were both here, both nights, studying, Inspector. Mother was at the choir practice so Nanny was here."

"Nanny?"

"Yes, Nanny. Our Nanny, of course. She's here for Hannah and not for me," Knox said.

"And was your father here?"

"He came home and was in the library. He likes to watch the television. Whenever we hear it on, we don't go into the library."

"Did you like Quentin?"

"Oh yes, very much," Knox said. "He was very kind to us."

"Yes, he was," Hannah agreed.

"Do either of you know anyone who disliked Quentin?"

Hannah shook her head side to side.

"No," Knox agreed.

"How about Hazel Weller?"

"She was in a wheelchair, wasn't she?" the boy asked.

"Yes."

"I didn't know her, but Quentin did. He would talk about her once in a while."

"What did he say?"

"That she was nice and she would cook dinner for him sometimes," Hannah said. "He liked her, didn't he, Knox?"

"Yes, he did. She was kind to him."

The door opened. Kirk trailed Mrs. Sare into the library.

"Inspector, the children must go to school."

"Yes," Caywood agreed. "Thank you, Knox and Hannah." He nodded to Kirk. "We must be on our way also. Sorry we've upset your household so early in the morning."

Next they crossed the road to Hazel Weller's cottage. The snow had been trampled to watery slush by the assigned constable, who was pacing back and forth. Caywood and Kirk spent thirty minutes there, and having found nothing, went to the Thompson cottage, where they questioned Walter. He was the seventeen-year-old son, who went to school as well as worked for the greengrocer in Cheamley. Also present were his sister Mary, a fourteen-year-old schoolgirl, and their father, Mickey, who worked as a mechanic for the bus line in Sexton. Mrs. Thompson worked in a tea room in Sexton. She had been employed by the Misses Knight but received more money for the same job near her husband's work. The Thompsons were the kind of working-class family who were one step above Quentin Stanley.

No matter what approach Caywood took, the Thompsons saw nothing, knew nothing, said nothing. Caywood did notice some intricate wood carvings in the Thompsons' lounge.

"They're Mickey's and Walter's. Their hobby. They use scraps,"

Mrs. Thompson said, and then added, "I wish they would make something useful. Once in a while Mr. Sare buys a piece. Says they're very good. I wish they worked for Mr. Sare."

"If any one of you remembers anything that might be helpful, please get in touch. We are set up in the church hall."

Caywood knew as well as Kirk did that they were wasting time and moved on. He glanced to the right, where the Clemsons were.

Just across the way Caroline Clemson said, "Please sit down, Colin. You don't have to rush off this morning." She poured milk and then tea into the cup in front of her middle-aged son. He sat and drummed his fingers on the breakfast table.

"Now, don't be so nervous, Colin. It will interfere with your digestion. Toast? Would you like one egg or two?"

"Two, please."

"That nice Inspector Caywood is out early this morning. He and that red-bearded sergeant are out making rounds very early indeed."

"Mother, have you degenerated into the village gossip?"

"What else is there to do? You're never here."

"Well, you know I'm working hard. You eat well. Have a nice home."

"Yes, Colin, you do work hard. Just as hard as I did to feed and educate you. And the home to which you refer was provided by your father."

Caroline's fifty-year-old son pulled nervously at his necktie and tried to settle himself down at the table. He thought the morning tirade was over, but on some days one could never be certain. He knew she was old, realised she was resentful of her current useless role in the community; yet there were some days that stretched his patience.

The large plate that she placed in front of him had golden scrambled eggs with just the kind of bacon that he liked best, and the toast rack was full.

"This is grand, Mother, thank you."

"You're most welcome, as you are every morning."

He smiled as best he could and attacked the toast.

"Where did you go last night?"

He sipped the tea and swallowed twice before he answered her. "I went to the pub and had a pint or two. You were asleep when I came in."

"Wish I'd known you were going. I would have come just for the outing."

Colin reached over and poured another cup of tea.

"No, thank you," she said as he extended the pot toward her cup.

"Aren't you eating breakfast this morning?"

"No, I'll have an early lunch. There's something amiss. I feel it." Her words trailed off as she walked slowly to the front of her home. Colin settled back now in privacy to read the newspaper and sip his second cup slowly. He was a serious man who taught music in the Rumsden school system and was the organist at St. Mary's. He filled in at other churches as well. Glancing at his watch, he felt secure in stealing another five minutes and a third cup of tea. Clemson stretched his lean frame over the table toward the stove, where he secured the pan and a second helping of eggs.

"Colin."

He heard his mother call from the lounge.

"Colin, come here. Something else has happened. Come see. I just knew it."

He scavenged up the last bit of eggs with some greasy bread and tried to ignore her. When she called the third time, Clemson dabbed the napkin to his mouth and his drooping ginger mustache. He wiped his hands carefully before getting the tortoise-shell bifocals from his short stubby nose into their proper case.

"Colin."

"I'm coming, Mother." He put his dishes into the cold water of the basin, where the droplets of oil froze to the plate.

"Hurry, Colin, they're coming to the door now."

"Who, for heaven's sake, Mother?"

"Open the door and see for yourself," she ordered.

When he opened the door, the men sized each other up.

"Good morning. I'm Detective Chief Inspector Peter Caywood, and this is Detective Sergeant Kirk."

"Come in, Inspector," Caroline Clemson called from her easy

chair in the lounge. Caywood flipped his cap into his hand and nodded to the middle-aged man with the wispy drooping mustache. He knew this must be Caroline Clemson's son but wished he weren't. The man's angular face was pale and his light brown hair was thin and crimped. To compensate he'd allowed it to grow long and curl behind his ears and over the back of his neck into his collar.

Caywood brushed past the son to enter the lounge.

"Good morning, Inspector, Sergeant. So nice to see you again. Colin, put the kettle on."

Clemson looked at his wristwatch. Annoyed at his obvious rudeness, the mother repeated, "Put the kettle on, please, Colin, and ring up the school and tell them you'll be a bit tardy this morning."

He turned slowly to do as he had been told.

"Sit down, please," Mrs. Clemson invited.

"Thank you." Caywood positioned himself across from the lady.

"The news this morning is not so good. Hazel Weller is dead, murdered. Her body was found in the river early this morning."

"I thought something was wrong. I told my son just a while ago I sensed something was wrong."

"Did you hear anything during the night?" Caywood asked.

"No, not really. At least I don't think so." Her arthritic fingers drummed the arm of her chair.

"Where were you last night?" Caywood asked.

"Here, right here, in this very chair, as a matter of fact." She thought a minute. "I'm quite certain I didn't hear anything."

Colin brought in a heavy-duty black tray with a more delicate teapot that he set on a table before his mother. When the cups were full and served all around, Caywood continued.

"Where were you last night, Mr. Clemson?"

"At the pub and then home."

"Did you walk by the bridge or along the river?" Kirk asked.

"No, Sergeant, much too cold. Why do you ask?"

"Hazel Weller was murdered. Did you see or talk to anyone last night?"

"Well, of course. Nigel Martin was on duty at the pub. Offhand I can't remember who else was there. People in and out, don't you know." Clemson spoke as calmly as they might be discussing the weather.

"Did either of you know Hazel Weller?" Caywood asked.

"Of course we did. She's lived in the village a very long time," Caroline Clemson said.

"Were she and Quentin Stanley friends?" Caywood continued.

"I don't know," Colin answered. "They were neighbors, just as we are neighbors."

"How on earth did she get to the river?" Caroline asked.

"We're not certain," Caywood went on. "Her wheelchair was on the bank. Was she in the habit of rolling about in her wheelchair?"

"Yes, she was, Inspector. She would go to the greengrocer's and butcher's," Colin said. His mother seemed lost in thought.

Caywood and Kirk refused an offer of tea.

"Hazel Weller went out nearly every day," Mrs. Clemson said, coming back to reality, "but she never went close to the river, and I did not see her yesterday. I wondered if she had shopped early, but then the matter slipped my mind."

The policemen expressed their thanks and left. Caroline watched them walk up the road toward the church.

"Why do you suppose anyone would kill poor old Hazel Weller?" she asked out loud.

"Probably because she was a whining pain," Colin replied sharply.

"Now, why are you staring out of the window? Want to see where the inspector is going?" She smiled at her son. "You're as curious as I. Hadn't you best go on to your work? You were in such a great rush earlier."

"No, Mother dear, I told them I wasn't coming in today." He picked up the tea things and carried them to the kitchen.

Caywood always felt a little better about the village after he'd seen Caroline Clemson.

"The son's not much," Kirk volunteered.

"Think you're right, Harry. What a shame. Such a nice lady. Did you hear what she said about Hazel being out so much? Contradicts what the victim said about herself."

"No reason to say anything but the truth. Mrs. Clemson's a straight person," Kirk thought out loud.

"Let's get back to the hall."

Caywood sat in the alcove office and let his head ache. When he reconciled himself to the fact that it was going to ache regardless of what he did, he decided to put the pieces of the puzzle together. It was apparent that some were missing.

"Why did Quentin have to leave early on the day of his death? He had seemed happy, not like a man going to his death. Where was he going and why? The buxom Amanda saw him cross the road at 2 P.M.

"Did the Adams children see something in the woods they wished to keep secret? Was it just a trip for forbidden sweets?

"He was last seen alive at two in the afternoon. He died sometime before midnight, beaten to death. He was not robbed and he was left in a graveyard where the body could be easily found," Caywood thought out loud.

"He had to have been beaten on the spot. His wounds could not let him move far away. He died close to where he'd been beaten."

He turned toward Kirk. "Why do you suppose the murderer left Quentin Stanley's body where it could be readily found?"

"Surprised before he could hide the body in the woods."

"The body had been there all night. Who prowls around graveyards? Why didn't someone report it earlier? Simply because Quentin had been killed earlier, elsewhere, and dragged there. The snow and rain obliterated the tracks, the earth froze, the body froze. Harry, we have to find the place where he was killed and we might possibly find the weapon, too."

"Inspector, nobody's going to leave a bloody place bloody for long. We've searched every place in Cheamley and found nothing but false trails and old secrets of no consequence."

"This is a secret place. I've never known such a closed society as this group of people. Yet I don't think the majority would try to hide a murderer. It sifts down to who was Quentin going to meet and why was he happy to go?"

"He had no lover."

"Except for Elsa Koch."

"A waste of time. He left her long ago. She either died or left him years ago."

"She died."

"Money?"

"He certainly could have used that. The only thing of value he had was that gold watch."

"We checked that out. It was a fake, a copy of some fancy piece."

Caywood laughed. "Maybe the murderer knew a fake better than we did. Didn't waste his time on something of no value. That's of interest."

"And now Hazel Weller to add to our problems. They're multiplying like rabbits," Kirk said. "She continued Quentin's game, whatever it was."

"I think we have to continue to look for bloody places," Caywood said. "Look, look, Harry, for bloody places."

CHAPTER 9

Silent Lives

Caywood turned the motor on and, to his surprise, it turned over promptly. He'd left Kirk at the church hall, sloshing in tea and coffee, to gather it all together. As he crossed the north bridge in the direction of Rumsden, he could see the investigation lines still in place while two constables chatted next to the riverbank. While the cat's away, he thought. There was little traffic. He made the journey faster than he thought possible. The transition between Cheamley and Rumsden CID was as abrupt as the increased pace of activity and the exchange of country air for the hovering mixture of smoke and hours-old salami sandwiches. Caywood's fatigue made it more noticeable than usual.

Upon reaching the office he went directly to the photography lab.

"Good morning, Dawson. Sorry you had such a bad night. Old Wick's the devil with new men."

"So I found out. Won't happen again." The boy smiled, rather grimly, Caywood thought.

"Have your photos ready, Chief Inspector. Pretty gruesome."

"Yes, quite brutal. They're not all this bad, though some are worse I must admit."

Dawson sorted through a stack of prints and handed Caywood a complete set. "I noticed the brake is off on the wheelchair." He flipped through the pictures and pointed it out to Caywood.

"Whoever pushed her down there had to be fairly strong. Dead bodies are dead weight, believe me."

"A man or two strong women," Dawson ventured.

"I'll take this set back to Cheamley. Good work, Dawson. Glad Dr. Wick didn't shorten your career."

The boy grinned and opened the door for the inspector.

Back in his own dreary office, Caywood put the photos in his briefcase and got Wick on the line.

"Usual blunt instrument, Wick? Is that what you're going to tell me? . . . Nothing else of importance? . . . Okay, I'm going back there now. If you find anything else of note, please ring me at Cheamley. Thanks, Wick. Talk to you later."

When Caywood arrived at the church hall, Kirk was ready for him.

"Here are the witness reports. We've questioned just about every and anything that moves in Cheamley."

"Good. Now, you and I have to take Hazel Weller's cottage apart brick by brick. Here, I've brought the photos. Put them in the file for the time being. Hurry along, man, before someone else pops it."

He took Kirk by the shoulder and pushed him toward the door. Kirk carefully put his cap on and smiled smugly.

The last time Caywood had been there before Hazel's death the cottage had been warm and appealing. Now the fire was out; the rose-chintz-covered sofa was no longer as cheerfully pleasant as it had been.

"Turn on the lamps," Caywood said. "At least she could afford electricity and make our job a little easier."

"What are we looking for?" Kirk asked.

"Anything we can find, old man, that we've overlooked before."

"That I know, but what in particular?"

"Any connection whatever between her and Quentin Stanley."

"Think she took over his game?"

"Good possibility." Caywood moved into the old lady's bedroom and switched on the bedside lamp. The bed was made. It appeared that Hazel Weller was awake when her killer came. Nothing seemed disturbed. There were neat embroidered linen scarves on the bureau and chests and on the bedside table as well. Her books were stacked in an even pile close to the lamp. All romances, except at the bottom of the stack were a couple of mysteries.

Caywood checked them out and realised he had read both before. He moved the bed quilt and searched the linens and looked under the mattress. A piece of china crashed, and Caywood knew Kirk was giving the kitchen his usual bull-in-the-shop routine. Next, he went through every drawer, inspecting the poor soul's neatly repaired underwear. He always felt like a peeping tom when he did this part.

Kirk came into the room. "Nothing," he said. "Nothing in kitchen or bath."

"Listen, Harry, I don't recall any storage space in Quentin's cottage. Surely there's some space in these miserable hovels for storage. Quentin was a cleaning man. Where did he keep his tools? Where did this lady keep her old treasures, too full of memories to toss, the family attic, so to speak?

"I'm almost finished here. Help me by going through that closet."

Kirk whisked through the three dresses and a blue overcoat that hung in the narrow closet close to a tall chest. "The killer didn't care whether or not she was warm, did he, Inspector?"

"Obviously she wasn't killed in here, and yet she didn't have an overcoat on in this freezing weather. What do you think?"

"It had to be close to here." They both sensed the truth at the same time.

"Get the lab boys and yound Dawson to Cheamley before we go into Stanley's cottage." Caywood expended three cigarettes, walking up and down the road waiting impatiently for his circus to arrive.

"Do you feel stupid and foolish?" Caywood asked as the door was unlocked.

"Embarrassed as well," Kirk admitted as they stood at the doorway of Quentin Stanley's cottage. The furniture, the fireplace, everything was spattered with blood. The poker next to the fireplace looked as if it had been dipped in it.

"What was she doing here?"

"She heard a noise, don't you think, and came to investigate," Kirk said.

"More likely she was here looking for whatever we didn't find, and the killer came to find it as well," Caywood theorized. He saw Dawson photographing everything in sight from every angle. "Let them finish up. Let's take a look around outside, Harry. Miss Weller had a key, or there's a connection between the cottages we've overlooked."

They circled the end of Stanley's place and came around the back. Caywood found a long branch and began pushing snow away from the edge of the cottage. When he arrived at the rear he stumbled and fell and disappeared before Kirk's eyes. The noise of his fall brought snow down from the roof so suddenly that Kirk nearly collapsed as well. He began digging like a dog trying to retrieve a bone. Down on all fours, he desperately scooped snow away with his bare hands. Then he saw Caywood's cap and dug even faster. He grabbed the inspector's jacket collar and gave a mighty pull. Then he began to slide and more snow crashed down.

"Help!" he shouted with every bit of lung power he could muster. "Help, for God's sake!"

Two constables arrived, slipping and sliding but strong enough to rescue Caywood and Kirk from the avalanche.

"The inspector's bashed his head. Nearly suffocated, he is."

"All right, Sergeant?" the taller constable asked.

"Yes, let's get him over to the church hall and fetch a doctor."

P.C. Tarlton, a giant of a man, carried Caywood in his arms as if he were a child. The inspector regained consciousness when they reached the hall.

"For God's sake, man, put me down," he insisted, but Tarlton carried him and laid him on a sofa as gently as he would have an infant.

"Well, Peter, trying to do yourself in?"

It was Wilson Wick.

"Where the devil did you come from? Caywood demanded in frustration.

"Just passing through, leaving some more papers for you. Now, how are you?"

"I'm fine, Wick, just stumbled and created a minor avalanche."

"Let's have a look at you. Just a bruise." He reached into his bag and coated Caywood's forehead with some ancient remedy that had been passé in the Dark Ages.

Caywood cursed as his head caught on fire from the antiseptic.

"Get him some brandy and prop him next to a roaring fire. He'll survive. You all right, Sergeant Kirk?"

"Yes, fine, thank you." Kirk hid the cuts on his hands before Wick saw them.

Caywood ignored the police surgeon. "Harry, get some men back there and find out what's behind those cottages. Get them some shovels. As soon as I warm up a bit, I'll be with you."

"Keep him in here today. Let him run the show from here, Sergeant," Wick said. "That's a direct order."

"Go to the devil, Wick."

"Do what I say, Peter. I've too many dead bodies to fret about already."

"Yes, sir," Kirk replied. "The inspector will stay in, and I'll see that he gets home properly."

As soon as Wick got out the door, Caywood reached for his cap and jacket.

"You heard what Dr. Wick said, didn't you, Inspector?"

"No, you idiot. I've had a blow to the head. I don't hear anything and what I do hear doesn't register." He grinned at Kirk. "Why the devil weren't we told about these storage places? Why didn't the local P.C. search here?" Caywood demanded to know.

"Tarlton just found out himself. The local P.C. is away looking after his sick mother. No one here knew about this."

"Except the inhabitants, of course, those paragons of knowledge and cooperation."

When they arrived back at the cottages. Tarlton and two other P.C.'s had cleared the snow to reveal five stone steps leading down to a door below ground level.

"I should have warned you, Inspector," Tarlton said. "There's underground storage to all these cottages, but the entrances fill up with snow. I just found out about this myself. Very sorry, sir. You all right now, Inspector? Proper lick to the head you had."

"Fine, Constable. Appreciate the rescue and your help."

Caywood went down the steps of Stanley's cottage and forced the door open.

" 'Pon my soul, Harry. Look at this, another world below stairs."

The storage room extended for about half the size of the cottage, ample space for another person to live in. Kirk pointed to a recessed door.

Caywood turned the knob, and the door opened as easily as he expected it to. There was a small electric heater, a tattered but sensible rug that extended the length and breadth of the room. Upon it was a double bed, next to which was a table, a bookcase, and desk.

"Very cozy and no problem for Quentin and Hazel to get about in. Good for them," Caywood said softly.

The rooms were neat and tidy with nothing out of place.

"The killer didn't know anything about these cottages, obviously, or he would have been down here. Harry, go over everything, thread by thead, brick by brick." Caywood shook his head. "Isn't it amazing what quiet lives people lead! Quentin and Hazel reached an accommodation of many things, it would seem."

"She knew everything he was up to," Kirk said.

"Indeed she did," Caywood agreed. "Imagine her grief and fear. I'll give her credit, she was a marvelous actress. Never let on a bit when I talked to her."

Caywood and Kirk spoke periodically but in the main concentrated on taking the rooms apart.

"Ah." The sound was soul-satisfying. Caywood let out another satisfactory sigh. "Here we are, Hazel Weller's journal. What a treasure I hope this will be."

Kirk was now down on his knees looking at the bottoms of the tables and cases he had searched from above. "This will be the frosting on the cake, Inspector." Caywood got down beside him.

"Right you are, Harry. Easy now."

Kirk took his pocketknife and cut the tape that held a large brown envelope in place on the underside of the table. It was relatively thick and terribly dusty.

"Let's get back to the church hall. Get Tarlton and our men to rope this place off and guard it every hour. Let's not let anything walk out of here."

"We're really stretching the men, Inspector. Tarlton's helping the lab people above in Stanley's and the rest are still at the bridge."

"Then call Rumsden, Harry, and have some men sent out here on temporary assignment. Tell Chief Superintendent it's a bad time to undercut us. He'll send us some. Fetch Tarlton, and I'll wait until you have him or someone to watch the rear of these cottages." Caywood carefully wrapped the material in large official envelopes and marked each appropriately. By the time he walked up the steps to ground level, there was Kirk with a young constable right behind him.

"Harry, I have but one question that you must answer before nightfall."

"Yes, Inspector. What's that?"

"How did Hazel Weller get down those steps? One wheel at a time?"

"You have a point, sir."

"Find the ramp, Harry, or find her wings. See you later."

Across the road, Walter Thompson cleared snow from the front of the greengrocer's. Walter Thompson personified sullen pouting adolescence. He shoveled slowly, watching the action. Mr. O'Leary, who owned the store, came out the front door.

"Walter, for heaven's sake, boy. I told you to clear the snow, not to make a career of it. Hurry up. I want you to take some packages down to the Knight ladies." O'Leary went back into his store. Winter vegetables were in abundance, and his trade so good he had thought about opening another store in Brewdon, but then he thought about contending with help like Walter Thompson and put the notion to rest. He packed some squash and two sacks of apples and nuts.

"Walter, please come in here now." O'Leary's tone was angry, but that fact didn't impress the boy. "Walter, come in here now. I don't know what you're looking at, but I'll be happy to let you gawk full-time starting this minute."

"Yes, sir, Mr. O'Leary. Did you want me?"

It took every inch of restraint for O'Leary not to strike the boy.

"Take these to the Tea Shoppe. And, Walter, if you're not back in ten minutes, don't bother to return."

Walter gathered the bags in his huge arms and made a rude gesture out of Dan O'Leary's sight. The boy passed Colin Clemson, nodded hello, and continued on his job. As soon as he had deposited his delivery at the rear of the Tea Shoppe, Walter crossed the High and into the rear yards of the cottages.

"Constable, how are you today?"

"Very well, and you?"

"Fine, just fine. What's happening here?"

"Miss Weller's been murdered. We're gathering evidence. Best move on."

"Yes, Constable." Walter continued to look around. "Who do you think killed her?"

"I dunno. That's for the bright'uns to say. Move along, boy."

"Who do you think murdered her?"

"Move along, or I'll nick you for vagrancy."

The boy walked slowly and reluctantly out of the cottage rear yard.

"Get back on the High. Now, pay attention. Get away from these cottages," the P.C. shouted.

Walter knew the constable had his no-nonsense voice on now, and he moved as quickly as he ever did. Twenty minutes later the boy arrived at the greengrocer's. The Tea Shoppe was two doors away from O'Leary's. The man was furious.

"Hand me your apron, Walter. You're fired. You're more trouble than you're worth."

Defiantly the boy threw his apron at O'Leary and called the man a foul name. When O'Leary came at him, Walter Thompson struck the man full force in the jaw.

One hour later Walter Thompson was in jail and a report of the boy's curiosity and escapade was in Caywood's hands.

"It's not related. He may be a strong boy, but he had no motive," Caywood said.

"Since when do omnipotent adolescent boys need a motive?" Kirk asked.

"You have a point, Harry."

"We found the ramp, sir. A strong one, made of wood with slots fitted for her wheelchair."

"Imagine that. Did she use it summer and winter?"

"No need to be sarcastic, Inspector. No, sir. We found a panel in the bathroom cabinet, false door that hid a makeshift lift."

"Shades of Sherlock," Caywood snarled.

"No need to be so sarcastic, Inspector, as I said."

"I'm going to be considerably more sarcastic and harder to live with if we don't wrap up this case soon."

Caywood moved back into his alcove, tossed his cap onto the desk, and pulled out his cigarette case. He lit one up and rested for a minute or so. A little more relaxed, he crossed his knees and settled into the most comfortable chair in the church hall. Kirk had pushed it far into the alcove and given Caywood aspirin for his aching head. "It's a gift from Vicar," Kirk said, and Caywood was gratitude personified as he saw the great brown leather chair.

The first pages of Hazel Weller's journal nearly put him to sleep. There were at least one hundred pages of a young woman's silly romantic thoughts and longings. Then there was a great gap from her youth until the time of her accident, which occurred ten years before her murder. Caywood tried to thumb through some pages too quickly. It was as if he were trying to get through the dull parts of a novel, hoping for something more exciting. He decided that he was not being paid to be sloppy, so he took another aspirin and started again to study the last ten years of a pitiful life.

The downstairs arrangement with Quentin Stanley had begun gradually four years before her death. It had been a slow coming together resulting from their loneliness and despair. Caywood read quickly and finally got to what he considered important. Two years before she was murdered, she wrote:

> Quentin finally confessed that he is associated with someone in Cheamley. He won't tell me who, but says the person is an absolute villain, someone he has known since his time in service. I've never seen him so angry as he was tonight. The boy whom he has supported for all these years is not his. He

was duped into thinking the boy was his child, the papers falsified by the mother, and he has struggled to make enough money to keep the boy, now a man, at St. Agnes with the good sisters. I never saw Quentin like this. He wept. He beat his fists against the wall until I thought he'd broken them. Quentin said that he was laughed at and then he said the man, at least I know it is a man, told him he was the father of the child. He told him that the mother had lied to Quentin, that she and this villain planned to foist the child off on Quentin, make him believe it was his.

Poor old soul, Caywood thought. He fetched a cigarette out of his nearly full case and noticed that he had been too busy to smoke. He took a long, immensely satisfying draw on the second of the day.
"Kirk!" he shouted. "I need some hot tea and more aspirin." When there was no reply, he settled back again and read every word carefully. He continued:

Had I been Quentin, the devil would have been dead. I told Quentin this, that if I were not bound to this horrible chair, I would help him put this devil to death. Quentin said no, that he had a better plan. He would not tell me what it was. I am writing this now while I wait for Quentin to return. I think he has gone to St. Agnes.

And there it ended. Not a word about the past two years. She had put it aside forever. He set the journal on the desk and stared and brooded about the whole nasty business. What did he know? Caywood asked himself. There was some kind of quarrel with a man who lived in Cheamley. That he had found out the child was not his. That he had been duped. But there was much more to all of this than Hazel Weller knew. Obviously Quentin had not told even her the whole story. The journal was a terrible disappointment. Caywood cursed as he left the comfort of the vicar's chair, left St. Mary's and walked up the road past the cottages trying to clear his head and put something together. If there had been any kind of blackmail scheme, Hazel Weller knew nothing of it or, if she did, she had sense enough to keep it out of her diary. The air didn't clear his brain, it only burned his forehead. When he turned back toward the church, he saw The Angels' tortoiseshell cat high-stepping in the snow, pausing to flick each paw as she walked.

Just like this case, Kitty. It's going to take a long time to get anywhere.

When he walked into the incident centre, Kirk came through the opposite door.

"Harry, you finally got back? I want you to read Miss Weller's journal carefully. What have you brought me?"

"The papers in that envelope were old service records, photos, maybe of some help. Here you are."

"I'll get down to Rumsden to the lab and try to jog old Wick into finishing his report."

The photos at Rumsden CID took two hours. Caywood hoped now it was just a matter of confronting the killer and extracting a confession.

The lab had done a good job on the enlargements. There was Stanley seated in the foreground of his platoon, all neat, nice young men preparing to be killed. There wasn't a clue as to where the photo had been taken. The handwriting that looked as though a spider had walked through some ink had faded into a few unintelligible bars and dots. Caywood reached in the top drawer for his magnifying glass and cursed age in general and his failing vision in particular as he fetched it out. There were four rows of men, packed tightly together on benches, each raised above the other.

How the devil was he supposed to recognise anyone all these many years gone by? he wondered. Caywood searched each face for some response in his mind, some set of jaw, some vague resemblance to those living in Cheamley. He saw nothing and decided to pack it all up for a fresh start in the morning. He'd go over them with Harry. Maybe his sergeant would see something he was obviously missing.

He rang up Crisp's and made his way through a maze of secretaries.

"That you, Eliza? Finally. You are surrounded by the Maginot Line. . . . Yes, I'm finishing up. Just one or two more things. I'll take you out to a proper dinner if you'd like." He paused and frowned as he listened. "Well, can we make it later for a drink? How about that? . . . I'm terribly disappointed. Who did you say you were having dinner with?" He listened, then said, "Oh well, Eliza, if that's the way it's to be, so be it." He replaced the receiver.

When he arrived at his flat on Clockton Row, Caywood undressed and propped himself up in bed with the newspaper and a beer. He became more depressed when he read a local item.

Rumsden police baffled by two brutal murders of a Cheamley man and woman. Quentin Stanley, whose distinguished service record is well known . . .

"By whom?" Caywood muttered sadly.

. . . was brutally murdered on November 17. His body was found by two children as they walked through St. Mary's cemetery. Mr. Stanley's body was not even cold before . . .

"Wasn't even cold?" Caywood said. "On the coldest day of the year. Lord, who writes this muck?" He read on in amazement.

. . . the body of an invalid woman, Hazel Weller, was found on the bank of Rumsden River. These two brutal murders remain unsolved. Funeral services for Miss Weller will be held tomorrow at St. Mary's in Cheamley.

He wadded up the damn newspaper and threw it into the trash. There was no point in waiting for morning. He returned to his office for another go at the photos.

"Morning, Inspector. Out with the birds?" the duty sergeant asked.

"Wish I were, with at least one of them." Caywood winked. "See if you can dredge up some tea, would you?"

He made it through a hall packed with various social refuse as it was at every hour and got to his office. One of the light bulbs in his desk lamp was out. What else was new? He tossed his cap toward the coatrack and missed it. Caywood cursed as he retrieved his old tweed cap and hung it properly. After rearranging the worn cushion in his chair, he pulled the envelope out and placed everything in the middle of his desk.

"Here we are, Inspector." The sergeant caught sight of the photos. "My, aren't they antiques?"

"World War II," Caywood said. "Glad we both missed it."

"My father was in it," he replied. "Has pictures just like this, a ton of 'em. Gets them out and points to this and points to that, just like it all happened yesterday. He has one just like that, all the men sitting on benches."

"Every squadron has one. It's a record for everybody."

"The one you're looking at, Inspector, was taken at Victoria Air Base."

"How do you know that?" Caywood asked, completely startled at the sergeant's knowledge.

"It's the *V*. See it there at the right-hand corner of the picture? My father has one. His squad was at Falconleigh, so there's an *F* at the corner. Both these air groups interchanged bad lots."

"What on earth are you saying?"

"My father says that whenever there were bad actors in the squads the men were shipped to Victoria from Falconleigh and vice versa."

"What could that have possibly accomplished, I wonder?" Caywood said.

"You know the military, Inspector, as bad as the police."

Caywood smiled. "Sergeant, I want to meet your father, today if at all possible. Maybe he can help me find my bad actors."

"I'll call him."

"Better wait until morning comes. Ring him and then set up a meeting time. Thanks very much, Sergeant." Caywood put the photos and clippings back in his drawer. "I think I'll catch a few winks now. Thank you, Sergeant." He closed the door and drew his long legs up as far as he could on the sofa. Exhausted, he fell asleep immediately, the dim light still burning on his desk.

In spite of being crammed into the sofa in his office, Caywood felt considerably better after three hours' sleep. When he pushed his way through the confusion of bodies in the main lobby that had continued through the night at Rumsden CID, he saw Duty Sergeant Alcott standing beside a forlorn white-haired man. The poor fellow sat on the brown bench against the far right side wall. He looked overwhelmed and yet curious at the same time. Alcott and Caywood saw each other at the same time.

"Good morning again, Chief Inspector. Here is my father, Albert Alcott."

"Bert to my friends." The man had a pleasant smile. It made him look years younger, and his handshake was firm. Caywood smiled back and felt that sense of enthusiasm that always came with every possible turn in solving a case. His stride was quicker, he felt ten pounds lighter, there was a sense of exhilaration that he could never describe to Eliza.

"Please come into my office, Mr. Alcott. Maybe Jack could find us some tea."

The son nodded. The father unbuttoned his suit jacket that was a mite too snug for a slowly expanding girth. His sense of relief was almost audible.

"Have a seat, Mr. Alcott." Caywood motioned to a sturdy oak chair that had probably arrived when the station had been built.

"Your son says you were at Falconleigh in World War II."

"That's correct, Inspector. I was there until we went into Germany."

"I hope you can help me by recognising some of these men."

Caywood pulled the material from his desk and displayed it to Bert Alcott. The man pushed his chair closer to the desk. He smiled.

"My, but these photos bring back memories." He was looking at the largest of the photographs, the one with the four rows of men. "There's my buddy, Frank." He giggled like an adolescent. "We were right terrible mates, we were."

Young Alcott brought in a tray laden with heavy white mugs of tea that he placed precariously on the edge of Caywood's desk.

"You forgot this, Dad." He handed his father a tan paper package.

"Oh my. Couldn't forget that, could I?"

The son smiled and patted his father on the shoulder. "I'll be back later to take you home."

Caywood rescued the tray and handed a mug to Bert Alcott.

"See if any of these faces mean anything to you," Caywood pressed.

"Oh, most of them do, Chief Inspector."

Caywood opened a side drawer of his desk and obtained his list of Cheamley villagers. "See if anyone on this list is in any of these pictures."

The old man laughed. "Well, it wouldn't be Charlotte Gill or Hazel Weller now, would it?"

Caywood felt his enthusiasm ebbing away like the tide. His patience was stretching thin. He smiled at the old man and tried to conceal his true feelings.

"Ah, here are some old mates." He held the list in his left hand and pointed with his right. "Poor old Quentin Stanley."

"Where?"

"There he is. He was a nice enough fellow, but no one really liked him. Some of the meaner ones played terrible jokes on him. Terrible, terrible jokes, they did."

"Such as?"

Alcott took a swallow of tea, as if to prolong his moment in the spotlight.

"He was in love with some German girl, and she told him she was going to have his baby. Wasn't his baby, of course. Could have been his"—he pointed to one man—"or his." He pointed to another.

Caywood got out his trusty magnifying glass. "Colin Clemson." Caywood suddenly recognized the face. "The other is Desmond Sare."

"Oh no, Inspector, that's Donald Finch."

"Certain?"

"Absolutely. Sly fox, he always had the luck. Like a cat he always landed on his feet."

"Tell me something, Mr. Alcott."

"Bert."

"Yes, Bert, tell me, what were English troops doing with German girls?"

"We captured towns, and we were hot-blooded young men. We did the natural thing. Then we were captured and stayed in camps until the end of the war. When the war was over, an old woman came to the camp with a baby. Finch and Clemson sold Stanley on the idea that it was his child. It was a great joke, they thought. Stanley got permission to take the boy back with him. I don't know how he got through all the government red tape. Neither the Germans nor the English wanted another mouth to feed, so Quentin got the child. It was retarded, poor thing. The woman died."

"Whose baby was it, really?" Caywood asked.

"I don't know, Inspector. It could even have been mine. Quentin had never been with a woman before. He was in love with this fräulein, and he believed whatever he was told about women."

"It's interesting that Stanley, Clemson, and the man you call Finch should all be in Cheamley."

"Finch was from Woodstock. He was very slick."

"He's in the furniture business now."

"Yes, I know. He seemed to like antiques even then. Stole anything like that that he could get his hands on. Sticky fingers, he was."

"He's happily married now. Lovely wife and children. Well off with several stores," Caywood said.

"And Clemson?"

"Schoolteacher and organist."

"That's about right." Alcott drank his tea, lost in his memories.

Caywood started to put the photos in some order. Alcott pointed his finger at another face.

"I guess Eddie went back to Brighton. Good old fellow. Now, Inspector, if you really asked me who the father was, it'd be only a guess, but I'd pick Edmund Morgan. Oh yes, very handsome. Easy with the ladies."

"Do you realise, Bert, that you've fingered the vicar of St. Mary's in Cheamley?"

"Eddie a vicar? 'Pon my soul," he whispered in disbelief. There's hope for us all. He was just a healthy boy then, but maybe some of our experiences put him closer to the Almighty. I remember now. Yes, he said he was a vicar, but nobody believed him. The Germans didn't believe him. We all laughed at him."

"He's so young-looking, still," Caywood said.

"Eddie never aged. He's older than me. I saw him a year after we were back. Looked exactly the same as the day we met. I have some pictures of him in my scrapbook." Alcott opened his package and placed a rectangular-shaped book in front of Caywood. He flipped a couple of pages. "Here, see, there's Eddie and me, and down here on the right is Quentin and Colin."

Caywood still sat at his desk twenty minutes after Sergeant Alcott had fetched his father. He was stunned. The enthusiasm had dwindled to a bare spark of interest. The answers had just produced more questions. He pulled out his case and hoped a smoke would get his gray cells synapsing a little faster. The day was young, but he felt as if he'd been digging ditches.

One long, sweet, satisfying cigarette and the security of the rest of the day's allotment started wheels rolling again. He ran into the hall and out to the desk.

"Has Alcott left yet?"

"Yes, sir. He's in the car park."

"Run after him. Get him and his dad back here," Caywood ordered.

He rang Kirk in Cheamley and told him to stay put and then waited in the CID lobby for the Alcotts to return.

Bert Alcott seemed a bit surprised that the chief inspector had summoned him back. He felt important. The day was an adventure.

Snow still lay heavy on Cheamley. It was as if the Almighty had decided to keep it white forever. Whenever the citizens shoveled away sufficiently to define walk from road, another load came down to defy them.

Caywood rang up Kirk when they reached The Angels in Green.

"He'll meet us," he said to Bert Alcott. "Let's find a table. If nothing else, sir, you are due lunch with high tea thrown into the bargain for providing me with so many suspects." He pointed toward the cat's seat near the fireplace. Understandably it was the only seat in the pub that no one wanted. It was always the only one available.

"Since these two murders, Sergeant Kirk and I have carved our name on this place. The cat owns the seat, but she tolerates us."

Alcott smiled that nice smile of his again and kept a firm grip on his photo album.

"Move over, miss," Caywood asked gently. The cat flicked her tail and did not budge.

Nigel Martin, the owner, seeing Caywood's plight, came over. The din in the place was unbelievable. Glasses crashed, the fire roared, people shouted, and the cat slept.

"You'll have to sit beside her," he advised. "She won't move. Fearsome temper. Eat you alive."

The cat opened and closed one eye as if to confirm Nigel's assessment. "Name's Jenny," he said and tried to pick her up. Her ears went back and claws concealed by fur thrust out like ten switchblades lined up for action.

"Don't bother her," Caywood decided. "We'll squeeze around her. We're accustomed to it now."

"It's the fire," Nigel said. "She likes the fire."

"Perfectly fine. Bring us a couple of pints and we'll have whatever you recommend to eat."

Nigel Martin nodded and made his way through a crowd of faces that were fast becoming familiar to Caywood. Kirk arrived and had sense enough to steal a chair in order not to argue with the cat for a seat.

"Harry, this is Bert Alcott, our duty sergeant's father. Bert, this is Sergeant Harry Kirk."

"How do, Sergeant? My son has spoken of you often. Looks up to you and the chief inspector."

"I've brought Bert here because he was in the war with Colin Clemson and Desmond Sare, who was known as Finch then, and believe it or not, the vicar was there as well."

Kirk raised his eyebrows.

"Exactly," Caywood said.

"What do you plan to do?"

"Just sit here for a while, eat, and see who comes in and what happens. Besides, we owe Bert a meal. I don't expect the vicar, but who knows."

"And if nobody comes?" Kirk asked.

"Then Mr. Alcott and I will call on the vicar and see what he has to say about Quentin Stanley—that is, if we survive lunch. If the food's no better than the beer, we're in serious trouble."

Caywood eased toward the cat when Nigel arrived with the food. Tray balanced on one strong hand above his head and the heads of the customers, he deposited two large plates and two glasses of beer.

Kirk looked at the contents of the plates and ordered beer.

"Looks grand," Alcott said, and began gluing peas and carrots to the mashed potatoes. Caywood attacked the chicken and as the first piece went to his mouth Colin Clemson came in. The inspector signaled Kirk with his eyes. Kirk turned and moved to the man.

"There's room here," Kirk said to Clemson. "I'll get another chair."

Colin Clemson's face betrayed him. There was a fleeting, quizzical expression of recognition, followed immediately by disbelief.

"Colin," Bert Alcott said, "it's good to see you after all these years."

"Good to see you," Clemson said with all the joy of Ebenezer Scrooge seeing Marley's ghost. The memory of Bert's blasted camera came to him.

"It has been a long time," Alcott repeated.

"Yes indeed." Clemson fumbled for time. His face was a picture that Caywood read easily. He was obviously worried about what Alcott had told the inspector. Caywood simply smiled and let Clemson stew.

"Ah, here's Harry with your chair and a beer for you."

Clemson sat and decided to play the game. "Well, Bert, I guess Inspector Caywood has told you that our old mate Quentin has been murdered."

Caywood sat quietly amazed at Clemson's brashness.

"Yes, very sad. Quentin was always such a backward sort of fellow. It's a shame nothing really good ever happened to him."

"Oh, I understand he had a lady friend lately." Clemson winked boldly at Caywood.

"Do you mean Hazel Weller by any chance, Mr. Clemson?" Caywood asked. "How did you know about that?"

Clemson seemed flustered. "There are always rumors in Cheamley."

"Not even her closest neighbors were aware of any friendship between the murder victims," Caywood said in an intimidating tone. "How did you come to know?"

Evasively, Clemson said, "I really didn't know. Just a guess, Inspector."

Bert Alcott laughed nervously as the tension between Clemson and Caywood was palpable.

Now Clemson appeared deflated as he recognised the trap he had almost stepped in.

"What have you done with yourself all these years, Bert?" Clemson eased away.

"This and that, Collie. His Majesty didn't train me for anything but killing."

Clemson knew better than to agree with him. He swallowed the rest of his beer. "Well, it's good to see you, Bert. Will you be in Cheamley long?"

Alcott, sensing his upper hand, looked questioningly at Caywood. "As long as the inspector needs me, Collie."

Clemson got up from his chair. "I'll tell Mother you're here. She'll want you for tea tomorrow. Can you come?"

"I'll let you know first thing in the morning if that's not too rude," Alcott said, "but I really don't expect to be here tomorrow."

"No, fine. Well, I must get to work. I'm glad to have seen you and hope that you can come for tea."

Caywood watched Clemson retreat quickly through the great doors.

"Why did you let him go, Inspector?" Kirk was incredulous.

"Because we have two more fish to get in the net, and I think he may be the herring, don't you know. Eat up, Bert."

Alcott started swallowing his food whole. He thrust his fork into the last bit of beef and it flew up and over the table. The cat did not open either eye, but her mouth, teeth bared, was wide open and in position. She swallowed it down whole and stretched her top hind leg into Caywood's thigh.

He rose immediately in response. "She's an expert on that. I have a series of claw marks in memory of this case. Ready?"

Alcott quickly wiped his mouth as Caywood pulled his cap down and tightened his muffler.

"We're a bit early for evening prayer, but I think we ought to call on our friend the vicar."

They plowed through the snow on the road toward St. Mary's. The snowfall had stopped; the road was empty. Kirk walked ahead of them and then waited until Caywood and Alcott caught up with him.

"Clemson's car is gone," Caywood said.

"Well, we expected that. We've got him on the run." Kirk thrust his hands deep into his pockets as the wind caught him full face. "Not much further, Mr. Alcott."

"He may have had to go to work. Clemson's an educated man. He'd have no reason to get involved in murder," Alcott ventured.

The housekeeper let them into the rectory. "Vicar is on the telephone. He'll be in directly." Before she left she tossed a few sticks on the dying fire.

The Vicar Edmund Morgan did not seem at all surprised to see his old friend Alcott.

"Bert." He put his arms around him and patted him on the back. "How in the world did you get to Cheamley? I lost track of you too long ago. Here, man, sit down." He pushed a chair close to the fire. "Sit, sit, Bert. You look wonderful, a bit thicker about the middle, but then aren't we all." He laughed.

Caywood and Kirk sat quietly and watched the performance. The vicar kept the conversation up at a rapid pace. Morgan passed an excellent sherry all around. When Caywood could not stand another joke, he interrupted.

"Surely, Vicar, you must know that I have not brought Mr. Alcott along for sherry and old jokes."

Morgan was surprised by the inspector's tone and eased forward in his chair. "Sorry, Inspector. I'm sure I know you have a reason for being here."

"Then I think we ought to get to a few facts. Why didn't you tell me that you knew Quentin Stanley long before you came to Cheamley?"

"For the usual reasons, Inspector. I didn't kill him, and the past had no bearing on his murder."

"Really? How did you decide that?"

"Because Quentin never harmed anyone. There was no reason for him to have been murdered."

"Yet he was; so there had to have been a reason." Caywood leaned forward. "And what about Mr. Sare, whom you knew earlier as Finch?" Caywood signaled Kirk to take notes. "You understand, Vicar, that you needn't answer any questions at all. But if you do, they may be used against you."

"See here, Inspector," Alcott interrupted, "if I'd known you were going to treat Eddie like this, and him a minister of the church, I'd never have come." He slapped his hands hard on the photo album secure in his lap.

"There's no problem, Bert. I'm happy to answer Inspector Caywood's questions. The truth is that for years, ever since I came to Cheamley and found out Quentin's circumstances, I've tried to look after him. Extra money, food, clothes, whatever I could get to him without the charity of it being too obvious. I've nothing to hide from the police."

"Did you always look after him, even until the time of his death?"

"No, I think I embarrassed him without meaning to. One day I just happened to ask him what had happened to the German girl's baby. Just reminiscing, I really wasn't even curious. He said the baby had died. I told him that I was sorry to hear that, but what hurt him, I think, was that I rather foolishly said that although I was very sorry about the baby, it was just as well because it seemed retarded and besides, it wasn't his responsibility."

"What did he say to that?" Caywood asked.

"He asked me what I meant, and so I told him. It had been years ago, so I thought it was all water under the bridge. I told him he was not the father of the child."

"And what happened then?" Caywood asked.

"He became wild, angry, in a rage, and then he began to cry. He was inconsolable. He came to church regularly, but he never took another thing from me."

"Did you say this happened about two years ago?" Caywood asked.

"Yes, about two years ago. He cleaned the church on his usual schedule. He came to church regularly, but never took another thing from me," Morgan repeated.

"Vicar, the child did not die. Quentin lied. The boy, now a grown, terribly retarded man, lives at St. Agnes Home. Sister Elizabeth . . ."

"Yes, I know Sister Elizabeth," the vicar said.

"Sister Elizabeth," Caywood went on, "told me that Quentin paid for his son's care for all these years. First, how do you know about Sister Elizabeth? And how do you suppose Quentin handled the expenses on the small amount of money he earned?" Caywood asked.

"Sister Elizabeth rang on the day of Quentin's funeral. She told me there was very little money left, but she wanted to send something toward the funeral expenses. I put it together then."

"Who bore the funeral expenses and burial?"

"Collie, Des, and I."

"And how do you think he paid for the care of the boy?"

"I don't know. I really don't know."

"Incredible," Bert Alcott whispered.

"So you see, Quentin Stanley had a terrible burden thrust upon him by one of your squadron."

"Oh my Lord, what did we do to that pitiful man? I had no idea," Morgan said.

"Was it your child, Vicar?"

"No, it was not," he said angrily.

"Vicar, would you identify some photos in Bert's album and in this collection from Quentin's? Bert already has, but I'd like you to identify them also."

Vicar Morgan was a bit more contrite when they left. Caywood bundled Alcott and his album into the car and headed off in the direction of Sare's Fine Furniture.

Caywood lit up and filled the tiny car with smoke. "I suppose Clemson will have told him about your photo gallery, Bert."

"No, I don't think so," Bert said, lowering the window for some fresh air. "Collie and Finch had a major falling out toward the end of the war. Collie didn't care if Finch rolled over dead."

"What was it about?"

"I don't know. One day they were mates, the next day they were bitter enemies. Who knows? That was years ago. I suspect they may have patched it up and become friends again."

Caywood drove on to Collier and turned west to Rossmore. When they arrived, they found that Sare was in his Rumsden office. "Should have called first," Caywood said, so they set out northeast for home and Rumsden.

"Just as well. I'm having a nice tour of the countryside and a pleasant ride home," Alcott said.

Caywood had checked out a map and turned the car up Watering Road onto London Street and then left onto Anthony Road. There were a number of fine shops, and Caywood kept one eye on the traffic and searched the buildings for Sare's place.

"There it is," Alcott pointed.

"Right." Caywood saw it at the same time. Let's find the closest car park."

The quality of the furniture was better than Caywood imagined. It looked as if Sare was trying to return to the days of individual custom production, but he could also see a mass line. He mentioned this to Alcott while they waited for an echelon of hirelings to get Sare.

"What are you talking about?" Alcott asked.

"Before the industrial revolution, every piece of furniture was handcrafted, beautiful designs. The middle class wanted to imitate the upper classes so that when machinery was available furniture could be made in a line production."

"Well, wasn't that grand," Alcott said, trying to humor Caywood.

"But there came a time when it cost too much to change the machines, so all the furniture looked alike again, while the rich folk had theirs customised," Caywood expounded.

Alcott was glad to see the man coming toward them. He went to meet him.

"Finch," he said, "so glad to see you again. If I'd known you were in Rumsden, I'd have come to see you sooner."

"Is there anyplace where we can talk privately?" Caywood asked.

Sare was obviously surprised, but by the time they reached his private office, he had composed himself. The man's office was luxurious, heavy oriental rug, exquisitely carved desk, and chairs of the finest walnut. Clean, not a paper out of place, and so were Sare's London clothes. The office smelled of success. He looked taller and better in these surroundings than he had at home.

Caywood said, "Mr. Finch, can you tell me when you changed your name to Sare?"

"Yes, shortly after the war, my father murdered my mother and was sent to his reward by His Majesty's courts." he said it matter-of-factly with only a hint of bitterness showing around the edges. "I wanted to marry and have a family. I didn't think we ought to pay a price above and beyond my father's."

"I gather, Mr. Sare," Caywood said, "you were sympathetic with your father."

"My mother was a whore and a thief. I don't know how my dad stood her as long as he did."

Alcott sat quietly and observed that his old war buddy was as calm and unperturbed as if they were discussing what kind of marmalade they'd had for breakfast.

"Whose baby was it that Quentin Stanley brought back to England thinking it was his?" Caywood asked.

"I'm not sure, Inspector, probably mine, but it may have been Collie Clemson's. Who cares? Stanley was an old woman. He needed something to look after."

"Finch, you really are a rotten piece of fish," Alcott spat out in disgust.

"Sorry, but I forgot you liked old Quentin."

"Yes, I did, and I liked you until now. I'm sorry you had such a bad life, but you've more than made up for it now."

"Was Quentin Stanley blackmailing you, Mr. Sare? Is that why you pretended not to have known him well?"

"Blackmail?" Sare asked incredulously. "That poor old sod? He wouldn't have had the nerve."

"Well, thank you for your time, Mr. Sare." Caywood got up to leave. "I'll have more questions later. Please keep yourself available either in Cheamley or Rumsden."

"Why, of course, Inspector, anything to get this business cleared up. Good to see you again, Bert." Sare smiled.

Alcott said nothing, but followed Caywood downstairs to the showroom.

"Too bad he's such a nasty bloke," Caywood said. "He does make fine furniture."

They pushed through the late-afternoon crowds to the car park.

"If you'll direct me I'll get you home now, Bert."

CHAPTER 10

Eliza and Angela

Caywood slid his car next to Eliza's in the park behind Crisp's store, a landmark in Rumsden. He used the back stairs and in the process passed a couple of young lads being pushed toward the ladies' toiletry by their mums. He smiled, remembering such embarrassing moments from his childhood.

Up the stairs he went into Eliza's outer office to confront Miss Pumstead, Eliza's protective dragon.

"Please tell Miss Crisp I'm here," he said as firmly as he could to any dragon. It took a full ten minutes for her to check, while Caywood fingered through Eliza's appointment schedule.

When the door opened, he pushed through.

"As I was about to say, Inspector Caywood, Miss Crisp is free now." She closed the door behind her.

"Dinner?" his face pleaded.

"Yes, why not?" She hadn't even looked up from the stack of papers on her desk.

"Eliza, what in the world is going on with you?" he asked.

"I'm trying to make a living, darling. One of us has to have some brass. Christmas is upon us, and that is what allows us to survive the rest of the year."

"You're doing very well, aren't you? After all, I don't want to be pursuing a sinking ship."

"Currently not sinking. Listing a bit, perhaps, but I must keep my eyes on the lifeboats."

"Do you know Desmond Sare?" Caywood asked.

"Sare, of Sare's Fine Furniture? Sare's Galleries? Yes, we handle a few pieces on consignment. Terribly good, frightfully expensive."

"What's consignment?"

"Our arrangement is if we don't sell it within a specified period of time, he takes it back; if we sell it in such an arrangement, we get some profit, but less than if we bought it outright to sell. We'd put a higher price on it." She read his face. "Yes, I agree. Why should a customer come here and pay more when he or she can go on Anthony Road to the source? Because we offer service together with a designer thrown in for good measure."

"Sare lives in Cheamley."

"The crime capital of the Cotswolds?" Eliza laughed. "You know, I have a few of his pieces in my personal collection."

"One would think a person who designs such furniture would be a very meticulous sort of chap."

"Not Sare," Eliza disagreed. "He's the money man. He does know bad from good and good from excellent. Sare has acquired extraordinary craftsmen and apparently knows how to keep them. Maybe his is the only game in town."

"What do you mean by that?"

"There are very few places in England now where a true craftsman has a place to work. Most furniture is mass-produced and is for the most part shoddy. Sare's stuff is priced way above the marketplace. If he sells one piece, he's paid his overhead for three months; that's my guess."

"Have you ever met him?"

"No, I don't think so. Maybe I have, but I don't believe I have. I have met some of his men. Good, hardworking men who know what they're producing is fine art. Some of it does belong in museums. In Sare's case he has some excellent antiques, furniture, clocks, and china. That's one part of his business. The craftsmen in his factories repair antiques and make exquisite reproductions. It would take a museum curator to distinguish the authentic from Sare's reproductions. His men are that good. Sare does know its quality; after all, he selected the men who produce it."

"Would he give up everything for it?" Caywood asked in a quiet voice.

"What a question. I don't know him well enough to say. People who do know him would probably say yes. Why so curious about the great Sare?"

"I think he knows more about the murders in Cheamley than he ought. He knew the murdered man many years ago. He and two others, all fine upstanding members of the village, even a vicar."

Eliza looked up from her papers, arching her eyebrows. "A vicar, my word, times are hard." She got up and went into her private bath off the right of the office. It was gleaming blue tile with thick, soft blue-and-white towels. It was the only bathroom he knew that always smelled of mimosa. Caywood watched as she combed her hair and put on a strange shade of red-brown lipstick that looked marvelous on her. He went into the bath and tried to close the door, but she was too fast.

"You promised to feed me."

"Provided you take me to Sare's soon. Where do you want to eat?"

"Someplace where the food is good and there are no violins."

They took his car, and as they approached Rumsden's most expensive restaurant he tried to divert her with more conversation about Sare.

"There, let's go there." She pointed.

"We don't have reservations."

"We don't need any."

"What you mean to say, dear Eliza, is that if I'm with you, we don't need reservations. They know which side to butter their bread on."

Caywood prepared himself for the haughty waiter who fawned on Eliza and dumped ice water on his crotch. He requested extra napkins for his lap and decided to have a good time. Past the consommé, past the beef and down to the mousse and coffee, he enjoyed himself. From her attitude he realised that Eliza was reasonably certain Crisp's was going to have excellent Christmas business. He got back to Sare.

"Apparently Sare, or Finch as he was named, is quite sincere about his work. The question is, Would he kill a blackmailer?"

Eliza said, "It seems to me that if you had enough money, it wouldn't matter whether or not you were blackmailed. What difference would it make? Pay the bugger off. Keep paying him off and keep your secret. But I suppose if he made you angry enough by his audacity or increasing demands, you would kill him."

"The truth is that Quentin Stanley was a threat to more than one person in Cheamley, and when they finished him off, they had to deal with his secret lover." Caywood laughed.

"Why funny?"

"It just struck me what a strange thing it is to call wheelchair-bound Hazel Weller a lover. What a surprise that must have been to the murderer. Imagine this pitiful woman trying to maintain what she considered a fine life-style. She thought she had a secret to maintain her. The murderer squashed her like a bug."

"More coffee?" Eliza indicated that the waiter had the hot pot in hand. Caywood appreciated the warning and pushed his cup away from his body and toward the smiling wretch who would pour.

When he brought the check, Caywood paid it without comment. Only when they reached the car did he speak.

"Eliza, if we do not marry soon so that you can support this poor policeman, we cannot eat at this place again. I will be existing on cheese and beer until I get paid again."

She laughed at him.

"Only you can afford Sare's Fine Furniture." He smiled.

He took her back to Crisp's and deposited her in her car.

"Go home, Eliza. Dinner will be on you tomorrow night."

"Time for breakfast, Harry." He heard Angela's voice over the water pouring from the tap. It was no longer the sweet, seductive voice of their early marriage eight years ago. Now there was a rasping "come if you want, I don't care" quality that was not lost on Harry Kirk.

"There in a minute, darling." He still tried. The water swirled a few red hairs around the basin until they disappeared down the drain. He swiped deodorant into his hairy armpits and put the plastic container dutifully back in its proper place in the chest. He wiped the steam that blurred his image in the mirror. His beard trimmed, Kirk reached for the blue-striped shirt that Angela selected in her efforts to make him into her fantasy version of a cinema star. He put it on and went into the bedroom to finish dressing.

Angela was frying bread when he got to the kitchen. God, how he hated fried bread.

"Morning." He reached over her frilly pink-flowered wrapper and found her cheek to kiss.

"One egg or two, Harry?" The cold voice again.

"Two please, dear. Any bacon?"

"Yes," she went to the fridge and slammed the bacon-filled frying pan on the burner.

"Angela, I'm sorry if a simple request for breakfast bacon makes you so angry."

"Request for bacon, dear Harry? I only wish I had some snake's liver to cook for you. I wouldn't want you to go to that marvelous job with an empty tummy." She poured tea into his favorite white mug and splashed it on his hands.

"Thank you very much. Why does every conversation of ours wind up in a fight?" He threw his cup against the table and strode out the rear door in a rage. She heard him gun the car engine and tear out the drive. Angela tossed her fat-soaked bread and raw bacon into the pail near the sink and burst into tears.

"Damn you, Harry!" She pounded the table with her fists.

Kirk vented his temper on the potholed black road that led to Cheamley. He didn't deserve her abuse. He had provided a good home for her, no philandering to boot. Why couldn't she understand it was his job that she hated so much that provided everything for them. A small terrier chased a squirrel across Kirk's path. He slammed the brakes and came back to reality as the dog scampered away. The only thing left to him was to concentrate on the job and wait for the next examinations. With promotion would come a little more money. Maybe that would pacify Angela, at least a little longer.

He put her out of his mind and took his frustration out on the road. When he reached St. Mary's Church, Harry Kirk went into the church hall and found some coffee and a cold stale roll. Then he went immediately to the Clemsons'.

It was obvious Colin was surprised to see him, but he tried to cover it up with a bit more courtesy than was needed. The Clemsons' lounge was familiar territory by now.

"Did you wish to speak to my mother?"

"No, sir. I wish to speak to you."

"Please sit down, Sergeant. May I get you some tea?"

"No, thank you, Mr. Clemson. I'd like your opinions as well as the answers to some questions about these murders."

"We've been through this before."

"Be patient, Mr. Clemson. I won't be long."

"I've told Chief Inspector Caywood that I was at a school meeting in Rumsden on the night Quentin was murdered. There were at least five other people seated at the table with me."

"Yes, I know. Our people have confirmed that, together with the facts of when you got home. Where were you Monday from noon on?"

"Working, of course, teaching in Rumsden as usual. A dozen students can verify this."

"Do you rotate in teaching? Do you move from one classroom to another or from school to school for that matter?"

"From school to school in Rumsden, four schools altogether. However, on Mondays I teach only at two, Rumsden Middle and St. George's Middle. All of this can be verified."

"Very well, sir. I'll check it out."

"I'm certain you will."

"By the way, Mr. Clemson, you apparently knew Mr. Sare during the war, as well as Vicar Morgan."

"Yes, and your Inspector Caywood knows the details."

"Yes, sir, but he had a few more questions for you. When did you last see Hazel Weller?"

"Maybe months ago. Our paths simply did not cross. It's been so long ago I cannot remember."

"And Quentin Stanley?"

"The same, months ago. If I saw him recently, we probably waved in passing. I know for a fact I have not spoken to him in at least a year, and probably longer."

"And Desmond Sare?"

"Desmond Sare?" Clemson asked incredulously.

"Yes, sir, Desmond Sare, or Finch as you once knew him."

"I cannot remember when, Sergeant. I am in Rumsden every weekday and frequently on Saturday as well. On Sundays I play the organ either in Cheamley or Rumsden or one of the local villages."

"You have not seen Mr. Sare in Rumsden recently then, sir?"

"Not that I remember."

The door to the lounge opened. "Colin, what's the trouble?" Caroline Clemson had entered the room. Dressed in a warm dressing gown, her hair done up in a wispy old-fashioned net, she still had sleep written over her face.

"Oh, Sergeant Kirk, I didn't see you. I've overslept."

"I've finished talking to Mr. Clemson. Sorry to have disturbed you, ma'am. I'll be going now. Thank you both."

Colin escorted Kirk to the door and returned to the room in a fury.

"Colin, have you told me everything you know about the murders of those poor people? Are you involved in any way?" his mother asked.

"No, mother, most emphatically I am not."

"You don't realise how happy that makes me feel." Her voice was soft and sad as she watched her son leave the room. She knew he was lying.

The inquiry into the death of Hazel Weller took even less time than that of Quentin Stanley. Dr. Wick gave his evidence, and Mr. Marsdon concluded that Miss Weller had died as a result of a felonious assault. Caywood and Kirk attended, together with Dawson and a few assorted police constables. Mr. Marsdon had a wretched cough that made his quavery voice even more annoying to those obliged to listen.

As soon as feasible the body was returned to the undertaker, who brought Hazel Weller back to Cheamley.

Her funeral was not as well attended as Stanley's had been. Caywood had not made P.C. Dexter attend simply because he'd forgotten. He walked slowly, fatigue written over him, into the church hall and sought refuge in his alcove. Kirk had managed a small brass coatrack rescued from the jumble sale and placed it behind Caywood's chair. He tossed his cap, missed it, and groaned as he stooped to retrieve it.

Upon the desk was Wick's report on Hazel Weller. He flipped through twenty-five pages and decided Wick must be getting old —he was five pages shorter than usual—but he got to the last page where the meat of the matter was, and read the attached note:

Dear Peter,
I thought you'd skip down to here. The old girl had her skull fractured in several places. Also, her legs were atrophied, no use of them since her accident. In other words, she didn't walk to the river.

Warmest regards,
W. Wick

Caywood smiled and tossed the report into his briefcase and went to look for Kirk.

"He's out, somewhere in the village," a young constable said, barely looking up from his papers.

Kirk was still a board man. He always made great unwieldy charts with every person's name on it. He had columns for dates, motive, opportunity. Caywood had given up such rituals long ago. They seemed to help Harry. He wondered where the Cheamley chart was. Perhaps Harry was embarrassed and kept it secretly at home. He had decided that certain things were obvious, at least in his own mind. Quentin Stanley was blackmailing Sare, slowly milking him over the years, and Sare was paying to protect his children. Probably, when Quentin knew the burden he had been carrying for so many years was not his, he upped the price. Maybe the furniture business was not as profitable as Eliza thought, or maybe Sare had just had enough. He decided to make a few discreet inquiries. Sare had stores in at least two places other than Rumsden. Maybe he had spread himself a bit too thin.

Caywood walked a bit farther toward his car when he saw Derek Adams.

"How are you, Derek? Do you remember me, Inspector Caywood?"

"Yes, sir." The lower lip sagged a bit.

"Derek, what were you and Rose doing when you found Quentin's body?"

"We went to see the bear. Quentin said there was a bear in the woods."

"That's not true. I found this." He held out a silver chain. "Does this belong to you or Rose?"

"It belongs to Rose. She lost it while we were looking for the bear."

"I don't believe what you're saying about a bear. Why don't you tell me the truth?" Caywood must have seemed like a giant as he looked down on an obviously frightened boy. "Did you go to Mayfest?"

"Yes," Derek said weakly, "to get sweets."

"And what happened?"

"Nothing. We came home."

"Was that Tuesday or Wednesday?"

"I don't remember," Derek said.

"Yes you do, Derek. You went to Mayfest Tuesday and Wednesday and Thursday as well," Caywood guessed. "What happened Tuesday?"

"Rose and I went to Mayfest for sweets. When we came home, she missed her chain and cross. We decided to go back the next day before Mum found out about Rose's cross."

"What did you see Wednesday?"

"We came back late. We looked everywhere in the woods, everywhere, but we couldn't find it."

"What did you see?" Caywood asked as he placed a hand on the boy's shoulder.

"Quentin was in the woods talking to someone. We heard them."

"Was it a man or a woman?" Caywood asked.

"I don't know. They sounded very angry, so we didn't get any closer."

"What did you do?"

"We walked back toward Mayfest and waited awhile in the woods, just playing."

"Why didn't you just go past them? You said Quentin was there and that you liked him."

"They were fighting. Quentin was being beaten."

"And you didn't go for help?"

"He saw me and told me to run away. 'Get away,' he said." The boy began to stammer and cry.

"What did you do?"

"We ran away and finally got home the long way 'round."

"Did you see Quentin anymore?"

"Yes." He hesitated. "On Thursday."

"Oh yes," Caywood said. "I know about Thursday."

"No, sir."

"What do you mean?"

"Rose and I found Quentin dead in the woods, and we dragged him to the cemetery."

"Why did you do that?"

"It was snowing, and he would have been lost in the snow."

"Derek, it would have been impossible for you and your sister to have done what you said. Quite impossible. Now, tell me what really happened."

"We found Quentin dead in the woods and we dragged him into the cemetery. When we couldn't pull him any farther we went for the vicar."

"And you did not recognise who was beating Quentin? Surely you know who it was, Derek."

"No, I don't. It was a man, but I don't know who it was."

"A man, at least you're certain of that. You said you didn't know whether it was a man just a minute ago."

"Yes, sir. I mean no, sir. It was a man, sir."

"Derek, run home. Sergeant Kirk or I will be by later to talk to you and your sister again. Please tell your mother the truth now, boy. You have no reason to be frightened. Run on now."

Caywood watched the boy run to his home and waited until he

was safely inside. He returned to the church hall and grabbed the first P.C. in sight.

"Please find Sergeant Kirk for me as quickly as possible and bring him here." Caywood walked up and down the church hall lobby trying his best to stay out of the church ladies' way. He saw the red beard coming.

"Kirk, hurry up, man." He went out to meet him. "Get some men and clean those woods."

They spent the next hour searching every inch of the woods separating St. Mary's from Mayfest. Kirk finally dismissed the men, and he and Caywood retired to their alcove in the church hall. Disgustedly they faced each other across the desk. Caywood brought his silver case out and offered Kirk a cigarette, which he declined.

"Harry, the Adams children lied. They well may have seen the fight or heard it, but it was not until the next day that they discovered the body. They were terrified by what they saw. Imagine their guilt when they realized that they had left their friend to be beaten to death."

"Poor children." Kirk sighed. "Too bad they didn't run for help."

"Why didn't they, Harry?"

"Because Quentin told them to get away."

"Or what else?"

"They knew the murderer."

"Or at least think they do." Caywood let the smoke circle above his head. "Lord knows what nightmares they've had. But what they said was that Quentin and a man were fighting. They left and found the body the next day. Amanda Fields saw Quentin in the road at about 2 P.M. The Sares' maid was angry because he had left early. The children saw him after school and discovered him the next day, late after school. What does that say to you?"

"I'm not certain, Inspector, not at all certain." Kirk had fetched his notebook and was turning pages rapidly to confirm what Caywood had just said.

"Never mind your notes, Harry, just listen to me. Why or how could Quentin's body be in the graveyard from Wednesday night, when he died, until Thursday afternoon when he was found?"

"If the children found him Thursday and pulled his body into the cemetery—"

"No, they didn't do that," Caywood interrupted, "they just couldn't do that. The murderer pulled the body there and was going to bury it. The children were genuinely terrified and have remained in a serious state of depression and anxiety, according to their mother. I'll tell you what I think happened, Harry. The murderer left the body in the woods and returned the next day to bury it. He dragged Quentin into the cemetery under cover of the snowstorm and he heard the children coming and fled. The body was there to be buried. Whoever the culprit is had a right to be in that graveyard. Everyone in this village could be seen at St. Mary's without any questions asked. The murderer belongs in this village."

"What a fortuitous snowstorm." Kirk smiled.

"For Quentin it was. The murderer hid the body in the woods. He could bury it anytime. He saw the snow and said, in essence, 'Now's the time,' or some such. The question is, Did the children see him well enough to recognise him?"

"Yes." Kirk finally put his notebook away. "Are they waiting to be murdered, too?"

"Or it could have been just as they said. They stumbled over the body after the murderer panicked and left it there," Caywood said. "They're so badly frightened I doubt we'll know anytime in the near future. There's another point. If the body was to be buried, it had to have been done quickly even under the cover of a storm and dusk."

"There was a burial last week," Kirk said. "An elderly gentleman who had moved away many years ago was buried here. Family plot and all that."

"So, there was a place prepared and everyone in Cheamley knew about it," Caywood said.

"Well, you've narrowed the suspects down considerably, Inspector."

"Yes, all good citizens. So get out your great charts and put it together for me."

Kirk blushed. "I didn't realise you knew about my charts."

"Get them out and give me an answer." Caywood pushed his cap down and left.

CHAPTER 11

The Fancy Pot

As he drove over the southern bridge, Caywood reached for a cigarette to light up his brains. He thought of going to St. Agnes to see that pitiful old man. Maybe he'd get there today, but the first order of business was Sare's store in Rossmore. He wondered what could have attracted Sare to a town smaller than Rumsden. Money had to be there for Sare to go to so much trouble. He went on to Rossmore, but once he'd found the shop thought better of it. He needed expert help to tell him whether or not Sare was making money. Eliza would do. She was as sharp with money as Sare was. Caywood had confidence in that. He stopped at a public telephone, rang her up, and she agreed. It was too easy. She agreed to come without hesitation, and he wondered why. He met her at the Rossmore Arms.

An hour later, with Caywood driving her Rover, they arrived at Sare's Rossmore gallery. Nothing like a quiet arrival in a village.

The outside of the gallery had only a circular window with a light from above shining down on three silver snuffboxes resting on black velvet. To the right of this minuscule display was the entrance, a single black door with brass plate and knocker. It said SARE'S.

"That's all it has to say." Eliza smiled. "But to speak so softly in so small a place as Rossmore does make one wonder."

"Just look around, Eliza, and let me know what you think."

"I wouldn't think there was enough business to support the shop here."

"They come in from the country, I suppose."

"Are you just curious about the furniture or do you really suspect Sare, or is it just me, Peter?"

"Come off it, Eliza. Sare is the only one in Cheamley with anything to lose, the only one with enough money to be worth Quentin and Hazel's efforts."

"You seem a bit too certain for me." She paused to survey the layout of the store. The furniture was displayed in mock-up rooms. The rugs were fake orientals of various patterns. By the time they had gotten two yards within the shop a middle-aged, impeccably dressed man appeared. He made Caywood's tweeds look second-class.

"Good morning. May I help you, madam?"

Caywood smiled. The clerk obviously knew who could afford the merchandise and went directly to the source.

"Just browsing, if I may." The Crisp voice put the clerk back in his place.

"Yes, madam. Please do. If you need any help I will be available."

She nodded. He walked backward a few steps, almost genuflected, then faded into an office at the rear.

The first room was George III. Eliza ignored the rugs and concentrated on the furniture.

"Well, it's an interesting assortment," she said.

"What does 'interesting' mean?"

"Strange, actually, the assortment of chairs, some early George III, some late. See the two armchairs. One is mid-eighteenth century; the one over there is late. One would fetch an excellent price, the other not much. Strange to see them both in the same room. And over there in the corner is an early mahogany elbow chair with caning. They're an odd assortment, that's all."

"What are you saying to me about this shop, Eliza?"

"Nothing yet. I'm trying to sort it out myself." She moved on into the next room.

"More of the same odd mixture." When she reached the last room setup, there were shelves of clocks, china, small boxes.

The unobtrusive clerk reappeared. "Anything that I can help you with?"

"No, not just yet. I may want one of these pieces. I'll look a bit more, if you don't mind."

"Please do." He smiled and disappeared. Caywood followed her into the last display area. They had been in the store for an hour according to his watch and no other customers had come in.

"The clocks are good, for the most part," she observed. "There are a number of French carriage clocks"—she pointed at two— "that are particularly good."

"Expensive?"

"Fairly expensive," she replied and moved past the clocks to a shelf of boxes. "This is a lovely piece." Eliza walked to the aisle and signaled to the clerk.

"I'd like to see this piece," she said.

Quickly the clerk unlocked the case.

"Yes, that tea caddy is what I'm interested in. How much?"

The clerk opened it and revealed a small card that described the piece and priced it at one hundred and fifty pounds.

"This is a relatively rare George III tea caddy," the clerk said.

"Yes," Eliza said, "maple wood and tortoiseshell. I'll take it, please. Will you take a personal cheque?"

"Of course."

He wrapped the caddy with great care while another clerk in the office discreetly verified with the bank the validity of Eliza's cheque. She watched quietly for the signal between the clerks, hoping to see how well they did it.

The second clerk came out of the office. "Excuse me, Mr. Quide," he said. "Mr. Barclay rang and said he'd take the chest."

"Thank you, Robert."

How clever of Mr. Barclay, Eliza thought. Her bank had given him approval. She winked at Caywood. Mr. Quide gave Eliza's package to Caywood to carry and thanked them for coming. A pleasure to have served her. Please come again and all that. Eliza smiled.

Caywood locked the parcel in the car. "Do you want tea?" he asked. "I'd like to go to Sare's other shop in Harton. We can get tea there or here."

"Let's move on. I have to get back to the store sometime today. Let's take my car. I'll bring you back for yours."

He drove.

"Thanks. You know, you look mighty pleased with yourself."

"It's a nice tea caddy, actually. Of course, you know Sare has been told that you and I were nosing about in his shop."

"Did it look legitimate to you?"

"Yes." She paused for a second. "But the quality was not up to his usual level. A hodgepodge, actually."

"Do you think he's earning a living?" Caywood asked.

"Not there, if you want an honest opinion. The quality is not there, the location is wrong, and the town's too small," she said.

"Yes, and here we are going to Harton, which is even smaller." He drove down a road that became almost too narrow for the Rover.

Caywood lit another cigarette and spoke through the smoke. "Sare has never done a thing without a reason. He is the epitome of cold calculation. These small stores are set up in out-of-the-way villages for a reason. The Rumsden store is the window dressing, I suspect. The largest store does legitimate business, a a cover for whatever is going on in Rossmore and Harton. The answer, of course, is to hide something in the open."

"Stolen goods?"

"Yes, hide what you steal in a legitimate setting among similar objects."

"Sounds like a sharp person," Eliza commented. "Sare's known for his ability in a deal."

When they arrived in Harton, Caywood was surprised to find that this store was smaller than the last. He parked the car on a side street, and they walked to a rather drab-looking building.

Unlike the small, posh exterior of Sare's Rossmore gallery, here there was no fancy round window, only a square glass front like any other store. The interior of the place could be seen easily because a nondescript rug not large enough to cover the rear of the display hung as decor. The eye was diverted to the interior of the gallery and away from the two chairs and table in the case. The furniture was undistinguished.

"Looks like a thrift shop," Caywood said.

"Not much," she said, "but let's not judge just yet."

They went in together. There were no fancy room displays but rather locked glass cases of china and glass with some jewelry. There was no other furniture. Eliza walked around from case to case. In the rear, rugs hung from the wall and made a backdrop for lighted cases of silver, each piece a little tarnished.

"Well?" Caywood questioned.

"Extraordinary," she whispered. "Extraordinary."

"Don't just say that, Eliza. Please be a bit more explicit."

"There's a Vienna DuPaquier two-handled pot and cover worth twelve thousand pounds!"

"Are you sure?"

"This is the real stuff. Belongs in a museum. You were right, Peter."

"Look quickly, Eliza, and let's get out of here before the word gets to Sare that we're here."

"Just a minute, Peter."

"No, now, Eliza. It's important."

"Oh my, oh my." She turned pale as a ghost.

"Eliza, are you ill? Are you going to faint? Do it in the car, for heaven't sake."

"Peter, let go of me! That's my Han cauldron. Do you see it?"

"What are you saying, Eliza?"

"That is the Han dynasty green-glazed cauldron that my father donated to Regents Museum. It's worth about seven thousand pounds."

"We're leaving now, Eliza." He took her by the shoulders and nearly carried her out of the shop. When they were in the car, he sped out of Harton as fast as he could without attracting the local constable.

"Now, tell me quietly and calmly what you said again," he pleaded.

Eliza was still sputtering. "If you dare ever to push me out of a shop or anyplace else for that matter . . ."

Hush, hush, dear. Tell me about the Han whatever."

She was livid. "That covered cauldron belonged to my father.

There was a nick on the right side that I put in it, and I remember every blow to my backside that my father applied for playing with his treasure. I know it's ours or at least it's the one we gave to Regents."

Caywood pressed the accelerator, pushing the car back to Rossmore, where he picked up his car and followed her. She drove like a demon until they were back at Crisp's.

"Use the phone on my desk, the 23 number. It's a straight line."

"Sarah," she called to the outer office, "get me Regents Museum in London on line 24. Get the curator, Mr. Startz, for me."

Eliza went into a smaller office while Caywood used her desk.

"Harry, we've really turned over a bucket of eels; they're slithering all the way to London and probably beyond. Sare is stealing from museums, maybe from private collections, probably stealing particular pieces for particular buyers. Miss Crisp recognised a Han something-or-other her dear daddy had donated to Regents. It was in Sare's Harton store. She's on the line to Regents now. Keep a close eye on Sare. . . . What d'ya mean, he's not in Cheamley? . . . Well, get around to the office and put some men onto his stores. Stay alert now, Harry, that's a good fellow."

He went into her side office, where she was still on the telephone. She covered the receiver with her right hand.

"They don't know it's missing."

"Why should they? There's a wonderful cleaning man who has substituted a reproduction made by one of his mate's extraordinary craftsmen who could fool a curator. I've got to run, Eliza. Thank you for breaking my case wide open." He kissed her on the cheek. "I'll be back in an hour. Meet you at your flat," he shouted over his shoulder and galloped down the back stairs, two at a time.

She left the office within the hour and returned to her flat and had changed to cream-coloured slacks and sweater when Caywood arrived. She had spread the coffee table with plates of sandwiches, his favourites, and some white wine in a silver cooler.

He kissed her and tossed a small book on the right side of the table.

"Open the wine, please." She held the glasses for him.

When he sat, she draped a white linen napkin over his knees and put a plate of sandwiches and a cup of consommé before him.

"Eat," she said, "and then I plan to kill Sare."

Caywood nearly choked. "What?"

"My Han cauldron. I want it. I have the scars to prove that I have paid for it."

"Lovely scars," he said.

"Never mind that. How do you plan to get my property from that bloody crook?" she asked.

"Eat, my darling. Come, eat now." Caywood teased. "What's the rush? The deed's done. Isn't that what you said?"

She threw a sandwich at him. He dodged it and pulled her onto his lap. "Isn't that what you said? Bloody nonsense to rush about."

"Yes, yes, yes," she gave in.

He kissed her and reached for a sandwich to stuff in her mouth. "Be quiet and look at that book I brought."

She got up and took it to the other end of the sofa. "Every museum in the U.K., I see."

"And Wales, Ireland, and the Continent to boot," Caywood added. "Now, we need your collection of art books and your best memory of what's where or, at the very least, where what ought to be."

"A very long night, I see."

"Correct, my darling." Caywood started cleaning the table, dishes in one hand, a last sandwich in the other. She followed him, putting the dishes on the table for the time being.

Two hours later he had a volume of lists, another half bottle of wine, and a great desire for Eliza, who was sound asleep beside him. Caywood carried her into the bedroom and kissed her good night. He picked up his book and his new volume of lists and closed the flat door softly behind him.

CHAPTER 12

Secret Places

Harry Kirk had gotten nothing more from Derek or Rose Adams and was convinced they knew nothing else. They had found nothing in the woods, no other weapon. There might be something there, but it would not be apparent until spring. Now his constables were stationed throughout Cheamley. He had the village buttoned up as secure and as tight as an old-fashioned glove. Desmond Sare had arrived home five minutes before midnight and was still in his house. Kirk's man was close enough to hear him snore.

Caywood put Eliza on the train to London, where she was to meet the Regents curator; as the train left the station, he was en route to Cheamley to pick up Kirk. It was six in the morning of a wet, dreary day.

"Miss Crisp has provided us with a Thermos of coffee, strong as Atlas and black as a witch's heart."

"Bless Miss Crisp," Kirk said.

"Ah yes," Caywood replied and plowed over the south bridge. The rain turned to sleet when they turned northwest to Rossmore. When they arrived in Harton, snow fell softly but so steadily that Caywood had trouble finding his way.

"Looks like a Christmas card, doesn't it, Inspector?"

"Yes, but I've lost my way, Harry. I could have sworn I was on the right road. I could barely get Miss Crisp's car through here. Yes, I'm sure now, this is the road. Sare's shop was right up there."

They parked and walked to the middle of the road.

"That is the shop, but it's closed. Look in the window, beyond that dreadful rug. The shelves are empty." Caywood cursed under his breath.

"It's still very early, Inspector."

"That's not what I'm talking about, Harry. They've closed shop and moved out. Look, there were cases of valuable pieces in there yesterday. He's left only the furniture."

"Now I know why Sare didn't get home until midnight," Kirk said dejectedly.

"Let's find the local station and tell the constable in Cheamley to get a warrant for Sare's arrest for possession of stolen goods. That will do for a start. Take the car, Harry. I want to scout around here for a bit. Pick me up when you've alerted Cheamley."

Caywood trudged disgustedly through the snow to the corner of the square. He turned right, down a side road, and looked for an alleyway behind the shop. He forced a gate open and made his way to the rear yard of Sare's. Tire tracks gutted the yard. He wished Harry would get back soon enough to get some casts. He saw a few bits of excelsior, one broken case, and some fragments of rope. Caywood got back to the road just in time to see Harry circling around searching for him.

"We need to get some casts of tracks in the rear yard. Get some laboratory people here quickly."

"Get in, Inspector. I'll radio Rumsden. The local constable says he was told Sare was moving his store and they cleared everything out late last night."

"That's obvious," Caywood said disgustedly.

"There's more," Kirk paused.

"I can guess. Sare's disappeared from Cheamley. Put out a description."

"I already have, and I notified the New Yard."

"Great, just great. What else wrong can we provincial cops do?"

Caywood and Kirk licked their wounds in the relative warmth of the car. They had polished off the Thermos of coffee by the time the lab men arrived. As per instruction they brought along the legal means to enter and search Sare's store. Now three small boys and two noisy dogs played havoc with the police, darting in and out doors on the road. Kirk finally chased them away.

It was noon before they finished. Caywood was wet, tired, depressed, but most of all angry. He drove Kirk back to Cheamley to eat out the constable who let Sare through their net. He filled the car with petrol just outside of Cheamley and treated himself to two packets of Benson and Hedges that he tucked into his pockets for the rest of a very hard day.

The next problem was to tell Eliza that her Han pot had walked away. How he dreaded that. Her train arrived in Rumsden on time, the only decent thing that had happened all day. She told him that the Han covered cauldron at the Regents was a fake.

"I thought the curator was going to have a seizure, and now I think I'll have one. How could you let this happen? What's wrong with the police these days?"

"Oh, Eliza, I'm wounded enough for one day. I will find your pot."

"Cauldron!"

"Eliza, I'd be careful in using that word. Say vase or pot and let it go at that." She slammed the door as he let her out at Crisp's staff car park. Caywood burned tires getting away. He sped to his office, cursing every mile.

He tipped his cap toward Sergeant Alcott to let him know he was in the office. Alcott had already heard the news. Wisely he brought the inspector a pot of tea and closed the door softly behind him. An hour later the photos were on his desk, photos had been flashed throughout the United Kingdom. Two vans had been identified by their tires. Sare owned both. Sare's shop in Rumsden had been searched. Now the net was drawing in, and Caywood felt better pulling it. All he needed now was patience. He lit another cigarette as he made his way to the car park. He took the quickest route to Cheamley.

When he arrived, Caywood went directly to the Sare home. The maid answered the door promptly and brought him directly into the library, where Mrs. Sare sat huddled near the fire.

"Chief Inspector, what can I do for you?" Her voice was flat, sad. She was seated close to the desk but seemed unaware of her surroundings.

"Mrs. Sare, where is your husband?"

Her voice was soft, her face seemed paler. "He is out of town. He left early this morning."

"And where did he go?" Caywood pressed.

"He didn't say. He left me a note saying that he would be out of town for several days. He would telephone tomorrow."

"Where is the note, Mrs. Sare?"

"I threw it away. My husband frequently leaves notes for me rather than bother me."

"Then you don't know whether he left early this morning or last night?"

"No, not really. I assumed he left this morning. I think I heard him leave early this morning." She was near tears. "My husband didn't kill those people. Why are you here?"

Caywood said, "We have reason to believe Mr. Sare was a receiver of stolen goods. The murders of Hazel Weller and Quentin Stanley are probably related. You must notify me as soon as your husband contacts you."

"I have no reason to believe that my husband will not be back tomorrow or the next day."

"Please call Rumsden CID or come to the incident centre in the church hall. I cannot emphasise how necessary this is." Caywood indicated that he would find his way out and left.

On his way to St. Mary's he noticed that Clemson's car was gone. Maybe that was not unusual, but he had a gut feeling. Caywood ran to the church hall.

"Ring up the schools in Rumsden where Clemson teaches," he ordered the duty constable. "If he's not there, bring him in."

Colin Clemson drove carefully on the ice-slick road across Rumsden Bridge, looking down briefly at the spot where Hazel Weller's body had been found. He drove steadily. The weather throughout the trip stayed as miserably wet, cold, and treacherous as it was at the start. He played glorious organ music on his tape recorder, periodically whistling bits of it as he drove through country roads and village byways. He was far beyond Rumsden, having joined the main motorway to London. Traffic was unusually light, or at least he thought so. How often did he go to London these days?

When he saw the police lights flashing, he pulled to the side of the road as quickly as possible.

"What's the trouble, Officer?" Clemson asked.

"Would you mind getting out of the car, sir?"

Clemson opened the door and cringed as the rain battered his face.

"Are you Colin Clemson?"

"Yes." He reached for his wallet and showed his license.

"Then come with me, sir. I'll drive and the constable will follow in your car."

"What the devil's going on? What have I done?"

"I dunno, sir. My orders were to watch for a particular car and license number and bring the driver to the station. Probably nothing serious, sir. Maybe just a message from home." The policeman smiled broadly and escorted Clemson through the downpour to the police car.

They drove back toward Rumsden and transferred Clemson to the local police. There was no formal complaint, Sergeant Alcott said. "The chief inspector wants me to ask you a few questions, please." Alcott escorted the man to a small office that was narrow, oppressive, and limited to absolute essentials. Alcott sat on one side of a small table; he had Clemson face him from the side away from the only door. The room was grim, and so was the business.

"Mr. Clemson, was Quentin Stanley blackmailing you?"

"What an absurd question. Of course not."

"That's your final answer, is it, sir?"

"Yes, absolutely."

"The chief inspector believes that you are the father of the retarded child born in Germany. We know Mr. Stanley found out the child was not his."

"That is not so," Clemson insisted.

"The chief inspector believes that you are the father of that man in St. Agnes and that you were being blackmailed in order to keep the secret from your mother and from the school authorities."

"Sergeant, you really don't know how foolish these questions are. Now, if there are no charges, I'd like to get on with my business."

"That's no problem. Only one other question. Are you on your way to London to meet Mr. Sare, or is it Mr. Finch?"

"No, I am not. I hardly know Mr. Sare. So please let me have my car keys."

"Not just yet, Mr. Clemson. As soon as the chief inspector calls, I'll be back with you. I'll have one of the men bring you some tea. Please stay here."

Clemson's face flushed with anger, but he stayed in his chair.

Meanwhile Peter returned to Cheamley where frustration was no less. Kirk's surprise was obvious as he looked up and saw Caywood. The chief inspector's face was as melancholy as the weather.

"Have you got everything under control now, Harry? Or is that a foolish question?"

"As much as it can be," he replied.

"Very well then, let's try to clean up this mess." Caywood signaled to Kirk to follow him. Five minutes later, after they had wound through the grounds, Caywood knocked on the rectory door.

"I need to see Vicar Morgan," he said to the housekeeper who opened the door. She escorted them into the study, where Morgan worked at his desk. The startled look on his face disappeared quickly.

"Sorry to disturb you, Vicar," Caywood said, "but I need your help."

Morgan motioned for the men to sit down. "How can I help?"

"I want some straight answers, Vicar, as quickly as possible. And I want you to know that you may be incriminated by your answers, so please do be careful."

"There's no reason why I shouldn't answer any of your questions," the vicar said as he put his glasses away. "Please, do go ahead."

"Vicar, are you aware of any thefts of objets d'art from museums? These various pieces of art are stolen and sold. The museums do not miss anything because skilled reproductions or forgeries are placed as substitutes when the real pieces are stolen." Caywood stared at him and waited.

"I'm sorry, Inspector. I don't know what you are talking about."

"You're certain you don't?" Caywood persisted. He waited for that fleeting change of expression on the vicar's face that might be a clue.

"Absolutely certain, Inspector. Absolutely certain."

"Vicar, I'm the last one in the world to remind you of your place in this world and in this community. There have been two brutal murders of members of your congregation. Where is your loyalty? You should know, if my presence here alone does not tell you, that I believe you know much more than you are saying."

"I know nothing, Inspector, that would help you." Morgan remained steadfast.

"Vicar, at this point in time I might be able to help you, but once I leave this study and our privacy, I cannot help you. You'll be at the public's mercy."

"I assure you, Inspector, I cannot help you. I know nothing about art thefts. I know nothing about the murders."

"Thank you very much," Caywood said and signaled to Kirk that they should leave. Once outside, Caywood said, "We've got nothing but suspicion on him or Clemson. I had Clemson picked up for questioning, but he'll be out as quick as he can reach a solicitor. We need to keep these fellows separated from each other, Harry. They are clever fellows, but we have to keep an eye on each of them. Let them worry a bit. Imagine the brass nerve of what they've done, but poor Mrs. Clemson's not to blame. I want to tell her before she hears it over the radio."

Apparently she was looking out the window, for she opened the door as soon as Caywood was on the step.

"Good morning, Inspector. Please don't look so worried. I've already heard, but I don't understand. Please come in."

She saw that they were seated comfortably and offered the men tea in spite of her anxiety.

"Mrs. Clemson," Caywood began, "your son has been brought in

for questioning. We think he knows something about a ring of
thieves who are robbing art museums."

"Oh no. I'm so relieved. Colin would never do such a thing. He
simply would not."

"We hope not, Mrs. Clemson, but we would not have brought
him in for questioning without some suspicion."

"But what has this to do with Quentin or, for that matter, Hazel?"

"I'm afraid the problems are connected. I'll drive you to Rumsden, Mrs. Clemson, if you wish to go, but Colin will be home soon if
he'll cooperate with us."

"I'm sure he will, Inspector. Colin is a good boy." She smiled
wistfully and corrected herself. "He's really a good man. He
couldn't do anything dishonest."

"Please don't worry, Mrs. Clemson."

They left her and pushed through the rapidly accumulating
snow.

"I need a drink and some of your thoughts." Caywood turned
away from St. Mary's and went to The Angels in Green, which had
been Angels in White since they'd been in Cheamley.

"Mrs. Clemson has my sympathy. Her son, whom she educated
to be a decent, honorable man, is in this up to his eyebrows,"
Caywood said. "That lady knows more about Cheamley and the
people in it than anyone else."

Kirk looked horrified. "You don't think that little old lady is
mixed up in this."

"Calm down, Harry. Course not. But she's seen or heard something and it's filed away in that bright head of hers. It may have
been there for years. It'll come jogging up sooner or later and we'll
know why all of this has happened."

Nigel Martin was stoking the fire when they walked into the
pub. He'd tossed another log on for good measure, and for the first
time the cat was not in what Caywood and Kirk considered their
seat. Caywood didn't notice, but Kirk looked carefully before he
sat down.

"What will you have, gentlemen?" Martin asked as he wiped his
hands on a white apron that covered a great expanse of abdomen.

"Two pints and some decent beef sandwiches."

"All my beef sandwiches are more than decent. They're dressed with tomato," Martin quipped as he left to fill their order.

Caywood groaned. "There's still no word on Sare. Clemson hasn't said a word, and the vicar's as quiet as a church mouse." Caywood tapped the table, waiting for his food.

"What happened? What broke up the partnership, do you suppose?"

"Money. It's always greed. Can't you hear old Quentin? 'I'm the one who is taking the risk.' " Caywood smiled. "The worm turned and got squashed for his brazenness."

Nigel Martin brought a great tray of food for the men. He passed a plate of sandwiches, thick crusty bread piled up with beef and tomatoes.

"Try these, Inspector. Made them for you myself."

"They look grand, Nigel. Thank you." Caywood took a swallow of the beer and choked it down. He smiled, waiting for Nigel to leave. But he didn't. He leaned close to Caywood.

"I heard they picked up that sissy organist Clemson. Did he murder them?"

"I don't think so, Nigel, but he's being questioned together with some others. Routine stuff."

Martin decided he wasn't getting anywhere and left.

"Where do you suppose all the loot's hidden?" Kirk wondered.

"The London mets are scouring the warehouses in the city, and there's no word yet. Harry, start twisting your gray cells. We're in trouble."

Kirk took a bite of the sandwich. Tomato squashed over the edges and oozed onto his hands. He was embarrassed. He swallowed hard and tried to clean up the mess he'd made. From nowhere the cat jumped up, purring furiously as she licked Kirk's beard.

"Easy, Harry. I'll get her. You're in quite a vulnerable position."

Nigel saw the problem and came to the rescue. "Jenny, Jenny, leave the sergeant alone." He grabbed her quickly, but her claws remained entangled in Kirk's beard. "She's expecting." Nigel apologised again.

Caywood laughed out loud. "Harry, she loves you. She thinks your beard is wonderful." He reached over to help the sergeant and a disappointed, expectant cat. Nigel tried to carry her away, but she jumped on the bench by Caywood and went to sleep. Caywood patted her while Kirk tried to regain his composure.

"Go on eating, Harry. You're safe. Now listen, suppose four men are in a German prison, starving to death, and vowing vengeance if they are ever free. One of them, Sare, is an entrepreneur. He probably steals enough to set himself up in a respectable business, one that will be legitimate but also one that would pay off more in the future. A calculating, planning man. A patient man."

"Sounds good," Caywood said. "We know or are almost certain that's what he's done, but we have to find the goods."

"Yes, but can you imagine how brazen this man is to put everything out on display?"

"It would seem so, Harry, but you know he called them reproductions. Who would suspect the real antiques and silver were there? The museums didn't even know they'd been duped."

"How much do you suppose there was?" Kirk polished off one sandwich and washed it down. He offered Caywood another sandwich. When he declined, Kirk took a large bite of it.

"That's what we have to think about. It took two small vans to carry it off. He dealt in small, valuable objets d'art, easy to steal, easy to hide. Hurry up, Harry. I think I know where he hid it." The cat thrust her foot in his thigh.

He put some brass down for the food and practically carried Kirk to St. Mary's.

Caywood entered the rectory study. "Vicar, here I am again, like the proverbial bad penny."

"Please sit down, Inspector."

"I wonder if you have a set of plans for this church."

"Yes, I'm certain there's one, but I don't know where they are at this precise moment."

"Well, maybe we won't need them if you could answer some questions for me."

"Of course." Edmund Morgan clasped his hands on his lap and

pushed farther back into his chair. The fire sputtered and was about to burn out. Morgan ignored it.

"Does this church have catacombs or any underground areas?"

"We have a basement, if that's what you mean, packed to the rafters at present."

"That's not what I mean, Vicar. I think you know what I mean," Caywood insisted. "I expect your full cooperation or I shall have to turn my men free."

"No, I'm afraid I don't get your meaning, but I'll take you into every area of the church."

"Well, that may have to do for a start. May we begin now?"

"Yes, of course." He rang for the housekeeper. When she came he said, "Please hold my calls and tell the ladies I'll be delayed. Bring them in here, and get the fire started again." Morgan buttoned his heavy brown sweater up to his neck.

First he led them throughout the church, down each aisle, into the choir stalls. They entered each door, probed behind every curtain. An hour and a half later the Vicar Morgan brought an unhappy Caywood and Kirk back to their beginning. The sounds of annoyed voices, noises they were, high-pitched, some rumbling, sounds from the ladies who were kept waiting for the vicar. They quieted when he came into the lobby. Caywood saw Caroline Clemson, bundled in a large coat and muffler. She leaned on her walker and looked so forlorn that Caywood felt compelled to speak to her.

"Blame me, Mrs. Clemson, for detaining the vicar. We have been searching for old storage places and the like."

"Oh, you mean like the storage room under the old organ," she said.

"No, I'm afraid there's no large storage room."

"Why, of course there is, Inspector. I'll show you," Mrs. Clemson insisted.

Caywood signaled to Kirk. "Tell the vicar to see to his group, Sergeant, and then follow me."

Kirk could tell by the look on Caywood's face that something important was about to happen. He came immediately.

"We go behind the new organ and down one level to the old section," Mrs. Clemson said.

"Does the Vicar Morgan know that place?" Caywood asked.

"Well, of course he does," she said.

Caywood signaled to Kirk. "Sergeant, stay with the vicar. I won't need you just yet. Mrs. Clemson is going to show me a storage place I believe we missed." He led her slowly where she directed him. "I've heard nothing about your son as yet," he said.

"I haven't either. I am praying that all will go well for him."

They reached the old organ site. "This is where it was, you see. Now, below here was where we stored other instruments, costumes, and whatever."

"How do we get down there?"

"There are two ways. There's a trapdoor here and a ladder down and there's another door behind the church. The old door still works, but it's covered by vines, probably blanketed by snow now."

"You stand still," Caywood cautioned. "I'll get this trapdoor open."

"It will be stuck hard."

"I'm sure it will be." Caywood pulled steadily, stopped for a breather, and gave another hard pull. He felt it give slightly and with one more determined effort the trapdoor pulled up. He fetched a torch from his pocket and flashed it down into a black void. Caywood saw a ladder and started down it.

Caroline Clemson didn't hear him approach, but quite suddenly he was at her side. She gasped.

"I'm so sorry, Caroline. I didn't mean to startle you."

"Oh, Vicar, you did frighten me."

"What on earth are you doing here?"

"Inspector Caywood said you were looking for storage space in the church. This place must have slipped your mind."

"Yes, it did." He squatted close to the trapdoor and called down.

"Inspector Caywood, please come up. I wouldn't want you to fall or hurt yourself down there. I have Mrs. Clemson here with me. Perhaps you'd best come up here now." The voice was threatening.

Caywood's strong right hand came through the pitch-black opening to prevent the trapdoor from closing on him.

"Vicar, I think we ought to escort Mrs. Clemson back to a safe area. I wouldn't want any of us to fall down there and break anything." He stepped out on the platform and pushed himself between the vicar and Mrs. Clemson.

"Vicar, I believe we have much to talk about."

Mrs. Clemson trembled a bit. Caywood took her arm gently.

"Vicar, you go ahead of us." The tone was an order, not a request. Morgan knew it. They turned down a graded walk to return to the sanctuary proper. Caywood held on to the fragile lady. Kirk came running, and the look of relief at the sight of the vicar with Caywood was obvious.

"Don't ever play poker, Kirk," Caywood advised. "Take the vicar back to his study and put a constable with him." When the vicar started to protest, Caywood turned abruptly. "Never mind, Sergeant. I'll escort the vicar. Please see that Mrs. Clemson gets home safely and tell all the ladies that Vicar Morgan is otherwise engaged."

He took the vicar by the left shoulder and forced him out of the sanctuary toward the rectory. When they reached the privacy of the study, Caywood spoke immediately.

"Vicar, it's time for the truth. Now, I'm going to tell you that I think you're mixed up in this business up to your eyeballs. I believe this enterprise began when you and Finch and Clemson were in service. Quite an extraordinary plan that you and the others thought up, probably as a joke. Then, when you returned to England, it seemed better and better. It took years to evolve, but once you had the craftsmen and the capital and Quentin Stanley's quick hands, the joke became a reality. It's only a matter of time, Vicar, before Clemson tells all. We have him at Rumsden CID."

Morgan looked startled.

"That's right, we caught him on the way to London. He's the weak sister in this group. He'll tell us all. You know that."

Morgan cleared his throat and started to speak.

"Don't say a word to me, Vicar, unless you're prepared to tell me the whole truth."

The man sat there, head down, hands resting in his lap. He nodded agreement.

"First of all, are you really a member of the clergy?"

"No." He sighed. "I took the identification of a young chaplain who was killed in Germany. My name is Marsh. I put my ident on him. He had no family, so it was easy. I kept up the masquerade for easier duty, and when we were captured they threw us all together. Clemson and Finch have always known me as Morgan, although they know the truth about my former identity. Finch and Clemson were officers. Colin knew Quentin Stanley from Cheamley, and although he was an enlisted man, he got through to Colin from time to time." The vicar shifted his feet. "We had a lot of time to plan, and we were angry. You'd be surprised, Inspector, how anger can carry you through."

"And you and Finch decided to come to this small village, where Stanley and Clemson had been boys, and use it as your headquarters."

"Yes, more or less. It was convenient."

"Finch got the capital. How?"

"Stole for the most part, anything that would build up enough for a start."

"Even the church offerings, I suppose," Caywood said disgustedly.

"A small percentage each month."

"Good Lord, man! What did you expect to do? Turn your collar right around and walk off into a life of luxury? What's your correct Christian name, Marsh?"

"Kevin."

"Well, Kevin Marsh, apparently you studied well enough to fool this poor congregation. Now, let's get down to it, and I want some truthful answers. Who was in charge? Who was the head man?"

"Finch."

"And who murdered Quentin Stanley?"

"Colin Clemson. Stanley threatened to turn us all in unless he got a bigger share."

"You know Rose and Derek Adams saw Quentin Stanley being beaten."

"That's impossible. They are confused children," Marsh insisted.

"We will see," Caywood bluffed. "And Hazel Weller?"

"I don't know. It could have been Collie or Desmond. I don't know."

"That'll do for now, Marsh." He rang for the housekeeper, who came promptly.

"Please get the vicar his coat. He's going to Rumsden," Caywood ordered. Then, to Morgan, "Now, get on the telephone and get in touch with your bishop. I want to talk with him."

"He's in Paris at a conference."

"Then get his secretary, damn it!"

A breathless Harry Kirk came into the study. "There's news from Rumsden," he shouted.

"Never mind, Sergeant. The vicar has confessed enough for us to manage. He's reaching his bishop's secretary to break the news that he's not a priest but an impostor."

Kirk's eyes widened and his jaw sagged slightly.

"Name's Kevin Marsh, been masquerading as Edmund Morgan ever since he picked up the identity off a poor dead chaplain's body. We have to get Sare as quickly as possible. I want you to get this fellow into Rumsden and keep him there. You, personally, Harry, are to see to this fellow. Get a complete confession." Caywood again rang for the housekeeper to tell her to lock up the church, then he got Tarlton and two other constables to search St. Mary's again.

There were two large corridors beneath the church that were lined with shelves and two doors opposite each other in the centre. Each led to a room, and each room was packed with boxes of silver, candelabra, various snuffboxes, and in one particular box was the Han cauldron.

Caywood took the shortest route back to Rumsden.

CHAPTER 13

Flying High

His telephone rang. "It's Miss Crisp, Inspector," the switchboard operator said. Caywood sensed her smirking as she said it.

"Put Miss Crisp through." He held the receiver away from his ear in anticipation of the crackling and squeaking which he knew she did purposely whenever Eliza rang.

"How are you?" he asked. He listened at great length. "It's police evidence. We'll take excellent care of your treasure. Just think how grand it will be when you do get it back." He paused and smiled as he listened. He was still listening when Alcott placed a stack of papers on his desk and motioned for him to sign them. "Now, Eliza, just consider how lovely the presentation ceremony will be at the museum." He raised his eyebrows. "Oh, they'll have another ceremony. Who will remember they've been duped? . . . Very well, dear, you have a safe trip. I'll see you tomorrow, right. . . . Yes, yes, yes, I will." He put the phone down.

Caywood looked up from his papers when Alcott brought Clemson in.

"Sit down." He pointed to a straight-backed oak chair. Alcott waited for Caywood to finish the paperwork. "I'll ring if I need you." He turned his attention to Colin Clemson, who sat pale, rigid, expecting execution.

"Mr. Clemson, I think we have all of this sorted out. We know that Vicar Morgan is really Kevin Marsh. We know Quentin Stanley, who was part of your setup, got too demanding. I'd like to hear your side of all this."

"I have no side. This is all nonsense. Who is Kevin Marsh? You're wasting your time, Inspector, and, I may add, mine as well."

Caywood turned and faced him directly. "Mr. Clemson, let me worry about my time, please. Your time does not concern me. You probably will not have to worry about time again, counting the years as they go by in your cell. So let's you and I get down to business as your associate Marsh, the illegitimate vicar, and I have already." Caywood waited to see if the name Marsh would sink in.

Clemson still did not flicker an eyelid.

"I have nothing to tell you. I know nothing." Clemson snorted.

"Let's start at the beginning, then. Let me refresh your memory. Once upon a time there were three mates who were wise beyond their years. They had another mate whom they tolerated because they could use him. They were thrown together, as it were, in the RAF and then they were stationed abroad for a short time at the end of the war and were caught. The men were Clemson, Marsh, Finch, and Stanley, all survivors in every sense.

"Finch developed an elaborate scheme after wandering through a few museums. There were very few treasures left in Germany. When the bombing began in earnest, Hitler had all the old people who were of no value otherwise in the war carry the paintings and whatever else on their backs into caves where they would be safe. So Finch had only a taste, but that was good enough to whet his appetite. When he was shipped home, his study truly began. Maybe he discussed it with the rest of you, but once the germ of his idea began to flourish, he contacted each of you."

Clemson squirmed, and Caywood noticed. He smiled and continued.

"Finch gathered up the men, dispatched you and Marsh to various museums, turned Stanley loose on all the private cleaning squads in London. There he learned the layouts, gathered building plans. Anything coming back to you, Clemson? Business flourished. You stole on order. Word has a way of getting around among collectors. An order here, an order there. This was an unhurried business. Sare's men worked slowly, skillfully. The fees were worth it. The collectors could afford the real thing as well as the cost of the stealing."

"Inspector, really! Must I listen to this fairy tale?"

"Of course you must, Collie. I have reason to think you're the Prince Charming of the story. You were the liaison between the collectors and Sare, pardon me, I mean Finch. You lined up the business deals. And you did a good job. Finch spread out to have a gallery in Rumsden, one in Rossmore, and another in Harton. All working, all sharing. Then poor Stanley, who was doing the real legwork, got greedy. He took the greatest risks and got the least. He threatened to expose the whole lot of you. You knew he meant it, so Quentin bought his. And apparently Hazel, his inamorata, knew about you as well, so she joined Stanley. What an unhappy story."

"Yes, it most assuredly is." Clemson tried to appear bored.

"Now we get to the good part," Caywood persisted. "Who murdered those poor wretches? Was it you or Kevin Marsh or Finch? Marsh says it was you."

"He's a bloody liar."

"Marsh? You don't know Marsh, you told me. Of course, you know your vicar."

"I know Vicar Morgan."

"Same thing, so to speak. Same person. Have a cigarette, Mr. Clemson." Caywood offered one of his allotment.

"I don't smoke."

Caywood lit one and took a long, satisfying drag. There was a knock on the door. Kirk stuck his head in. "Sorry to interrupt. Wanted you to know I'm back with Marsh."

"Fine. Be with you soon."

Kirk withdrew his head like a turtle and closed the door.

"Now, back to you, Mr. Clemson. Anything to say?"

"Nothing."

"Well, maybe I'll let you think about it for a while. Alcott!" he shouted. "Take care of Mr. Clemson, and ask Kirk to bring Kevin Marsh into the side room."

Obviously they had passed each other in the hallway, but the expression on the vicar's face remained the same, calm, placid. The pair had been actors for many years now; a few policemen were not going to crack their facades.

"Sit down, Vicar. Let's you and I have a bit of a jaw." Caywood pointed to a chair opposite him in the small interrogation room.

Marsh smirked. "Sorry I can't offer you tea."

"Well, we enjoyed your hospitality when you were in a position to offer it. Now, let's get back to the business at hand. You're going to be sent away for quite a while, if I'm any judge. You'll be too old by the time you get out to do anything except maybe collect your pension, and I doubt you'll be eligible for that."

"Oh, I know my prayers pretty well, and I know how to organise ladies' committees. You'd be surprised by my administrative skills. I may not be going back to St. Mary's, but I'll land on my feet. It's something I do quite well, actually. I didn't murder Quentin or the Weller woman. I'll get out of this."

Caywood smiled at Marsh's brazenness. "Let me tell you this. There's a lady of whom I am very fond. You and your gang walked off with one of her pretty playthings. She is not going to forgive me until I got it back for her. Somehow or another she thought it was in Regents Museum because that's where her daddy put it, but quite unexpectedly she saw it in Sare's gallery in the metropolis of Harton. We found her little treasure in your church. Now it's police evidence and will remain so until this matter is cleared up. She's quite angry about that. I have a feeling she'll continue to be angry until I get it back to her. Let me tell you, Vicar, the longer I am away from her, the angrier I will become. So, where is Sare?"

"I have no idea." Marsh drummed his fingers on the table that separated him from Caywood.

"Vicar, you'd better start getting some ideas, believe me. I want the whole story. Stolen goods were found in your church."

"There's nothing to tell. Not any more than I've told you. I'm not a thief and I am most certainly not a murderer."

"Yes, yes, yes. Now, let's hear something new. Start with your discharge from the RAF."

"Inspector, that's all a matter of record, which you have in hand."

"Not quite. Edmund Morgan was killed and you took his tags and became Morgan and were captured."

"Bang on target, Inspector."

"So take me forward. You met Finch and Stanley and ultimately Clemson in prison camp."

"Exactly."

"Take it from there."

"Sorry, Inspector. Nothing more to tell."

Caywood buzzed for Alcott to take Marsh downstairs. "Perhaps a little rest will help your memory."

They met at an abandoned country church at the edge of Rossmore. Sare no longer looked like a successful businessman. A knit cap covered his forehead and ears, and his gray trousers were stuffed into black boots. He shifted uneasily from one foot to the other.

"Everything settled now, Joe?" he asked.

"Yes, sir, Mr. Sare. All the merchandise is stored, so to speak. The police will never find your special stock. I've taken care of it personally."

"Thank you, Joe. Please take care of my wife and children until I send for them."

"Yes, sir. You can count on me. They've got Mr. Clemson and the vicar."

"Yes, I know. I'll be in touch as soon as I can."

Sare took the wheel from Joe Ringel and waved good-bye. He watched Ringel getting into the gallery van through the rear mirror. Driving slowly through the countryside now that winter had really set in was a pleasure Sare had not known in years. He enjoyed what he was doing in spite of his world crashing around him. He would go slowly and steadily and not attract attention. Periodically reality rushed back upon him and he cursed Stanley for his greed and the others for their hysterical reaction. He could have handled Quentin, but he hadn't been able to control their panic. He thought about the children and regretted that he would miss them at Christmas, but there would be other good times in the future if he could get away. He patted the case on the seat next to him and eased the car down the secluded country road.

Two hours of lonely driving left him drowsy and hungry. The road was amazingly clear of snow. Now it was three o'clock the sky was growing dark rapidly. Sare forgot fatigue and knew he had to reach the fishing village before midnight, or the boat would leave. He reached over to the seat beside him, where his left hand struck a packet of sandwiches. He fumbled one and gulped it down, realising how this terrible anxiety had made him hungry. He had to concentrate on the roads and the steep climbs that twisted up and then precipitously down. Another hour and he would be safe.

Caywood heard the alarm and rushed to the cells downstairs, where he found Marsh grappling with the duty constable. Marsh fought like a wild man. Kirk and Alcott arrived in time to help Caywood pull Marsh off the constable.

"Throw him into that cell and cuff him to the bench. If he tries to get away again, he'll have to cart some baggage along with him."

Caywood looked at Clemson, who was as pale as a day-old corpse and stood flattened against the back wall of his cell.

"I believe we must have had some kind of confrontation here between them," Caywood said. "Constable, unlock this cell. Detective Sergeant Kirk and I will be responsible for this man. Come on, Clemson, up to my office."

The man was still pale and now shaking a bit when he sat opposite Caywood. Kirk leaned against the gray file at the rear of the office.

"Now is the time to talk, Collie. We may not be able to keep him away from you next time. He knows where the keys are and he thinks he's strong enough to get them. It's time for you to help us. My patience is just about at its end. If you expect me to help you, then start answering my questions now."

Clemson sat rigidly against the oak chair and bit his lower lip. The man looked sick, and Caywood decided to take advantage of it.

"Now, Collie, start talking now," Caywood demanded. "What did Stanley do?"

The man's face sagged. Suddenly he looked seventy years old. "Stanley did the stealing. He was on the cleaning team of nearly every museum in England. He filled in or arranged to be at a particular gallery when we needed a specific item." Once he started, Clemson let the words fall out rapidly. Caywood did not interrupt.

"I took the orders. I met every month with private collectors. They knew where I'd be. They sought me out. Then Sare would produce a duplicate. I believe he had a colour photograph of every objet d'art in this country and in France and Germany. When the repro was ready, Stanley went to work, substituted the duplicate, and brought the original to Cheamley."

Kirk quietly shifted his feet in the background. Caywood held his breath.

"Then Eddie went to Hazel's to give her Quentin's commission and pick up whatever Quentin had stolen."

"And then?" Caywood asked.

"I would arrange for the collector to go with me to church wherever I played and pick up what he had ordered."

"And the money?"

"I took it to Sare, who kept the books and divided it up after expenses."

"You know Sare has left and probably taken all the money with him," Caywood said.

Clemson began to sweat. His hands were trembling.

"Sergeant, get Clemson some tea, please."

"Right."

The man just sat there in front of Caywood. He was close to fainting. He gulped the sweet tea that Kirk put before him.

"Alcott's bringing more tea and some buns," Kirk said.

"Good. Now, let's get back to it, Collie. Where is Sare going?"

"I think he might be driving to a small fishing village. It's not far from Boscastle, at least that's the nearest place."

Caywood said, "Get Alcott to put this man in a cell up here away from Kevin Marsh. Then get a crew and arrange for an aircraft." He turned back to Clemson. "Remember, I expect the rest of the details when I get back."

"There's no landing area anywhere near there, Inspector."

"We'll lose him if we don't get down there in a hurry. Now, Harry, surely there's a landing field closer to Sare than we are. Arrange for a 'copter and have the nearest station provide us with a car and a driver who knows the area. And tell Alcott to secure Clemson. He's turned into a national treasure."

Caywood found an extra sweater and muffler to get him through what he expected to be a cold, long journey. He swapped street shoes for boots and waited for Kirk to join him in the Rumsden CID car park. Once together, they drove furiously to the local airfield, which consisted of a hangar, a small tower, and a lethargic attendant. The police pilot was waiting. They were up in less than ten minutes and nearly frozen in fifteen. Caywood heard Kirk's teeth chatter. The farther they flew, the colder it got. When he could stand the noise of Kirk's teeth no longer, Caywood took pity on Kirk and gave him his woolen scarf. The pilot pointed down to an isolated gray slab in the middle of a forest that signal lights outlined. Caywood didn't understand and couldn't care less how it worked as long as the 'copter went down and landed safely.

A uniformed constable was there as soon as Caywood stepped onto the pad.

"Copperfield, sir." He led Caywood and Kirk to his car.

"We'll wait for the pilot to secure the helicopter and take him along with us. It'll be a sardine drill, but we'll make it. Let's drop the pilot off at the closest inn and meet him there later. We need him thawed out for the ride home," Caywood said.

When his patience couldn't stand it any longer, he shouted at the pilot to "bloody well get a move on." Copperfield jammed them into his official vehicle and threaded it down a precipice on a road that was barely wider than a footpath. He got them safely down as Caywood tried to put the return trip out of his mind.

When they reached The Silver Chalice, Caywood made them stop long enough for something to drink. As they sat at a long black table at the rear of the inn, the constable spread maps before them. Caywood gave Copperfield some photos of Sare.

"Never saw him around here," the constable said.

"He has some kind of cottage up here, off the beaten path so to speak." Caywood laughed. "Forgive me, Constable, but this whole place is off the beaten path as far as I'm concerned."

"Yes, sir," Copperfield said, "but it's home and lovely in summer. My wife packed us a Thermos to take along."

Kirk allowed how grateful he was as he scrutinised the maps.

"Now, here's a possibility," Copperfield said. "I remember some houses here and a single cottage beyond that spot. Stumbled on it when my boy and I went hiking last summer."

"Can we get there?"

"Yes, I think so. We may have to hike a bit, but I think we can make it. There's bound to be a road. We'll find it."

"Drink up, Harry. We're ready for a lovely winter's walk."

They rode like the proverbial peas, warm at last, headed toward the end of the earth as far as Caywood was concerned. The pace was slow, but safe as Copperfield said. He knew the way into this wilderness; therefore, Caywood remained silent, though impatient.

Just as he thought they would plunge into the sea, Copperfield slowed the car to a crawl and pointed to a cottage below them. "It's the only one in the area not occupied by a local." There was no smoke nor any lantern light. "This is as far as we can drive. It's on foot from here." Copperfield gave Caywood and Kirk torches. "Get out here and wait for me. I'll push the car off the road. Give me a hand, Sergeant."

Caywood looked up to thank the moon as it shone on the snow and lighted the landscape. It was an extraordinarily beautiful place, so peaceful for such treacherous business.

Copperfield and Kirk came out of the woods.

"Ready, Inspector?"

"Yes. Harry, keep your torch down," Caywood ordered.

"Sorry, sir," Kirk replied.

"Walk down slowly," Copperfield advised, "one foot at a time, and you'll be safe."

"Is there another road out?" Caywood asked.

"No, only water."

"Well, that's frozen, isn't it, so that takes care of that route," Caywood said.

"Afraid not, Inspector. The stream has a powerful current and doesn't freeze usually until late December or January. It flows into a small but magnificent waterfall. Stop for a second. Maybe you

can hear it. Listen, there it is. And then it flows into a larger river
and then out to sea."

Kirk was grateful for the rest while Caywood and the constable
listened to water crashing over rocks.

"I don't think your man has gotten here yet," Copperfield said.

"I agree. The question is, Is this where he's going?" Caywood
said.

"If I planned to escape the world," Kirk gasped, "this would be
the place."

"That's what I'm counting on, Harry. Obviously he's going to
meet someone with a boat or he has one hidden here."

The path became a little gentler and stretched out flat into the
clearing where the cottage was. Kirk sighed his relief audibly.

"I agree, Harry," Caywood whispered. "Let's take a look
around. Keep the torches down." Caywood and Copperfield
started around the front while Kirk took the rear. They found
nothing.

"We'll wait until dawn. If he's not here by then we'll go back to
Rumsden," Caywood said. "Harry, you and Copperfield catch
forty winks while I take watch. Let's get to the rear and get in that
shed for a little relief from this wind."

Caywood crouched against the shed door and heard Kirk snor-
ing five minutes later. He thought that his sergeant would probably sleep through an earthquake. He listened as acutely as he
could. The day had been a long one, so long that he could not recall
what his bed looked like. Now here he was in the middle of a
wilderness, waiting for someone who might never come and who
was probably clever enough to be in a warm bed in Paris or
Amsterdam. He glanced at his watch, ten to midnight. The sound
of the distant water was lulling him to sleep, and he fought against
it. He thought he heard Kirk turning in the shed; then he realised
there were footsteps on the path, and he saw a light flickering
through the woods.

Caywood rapped gently on the shed door and whispered, "Look
alive, our man is coming."

Kirk eased out of the shed, followed by Copperfield. Caywood
signaled them to go in opposite directions. He wished Sare had

waited until dawn. Clouds hid the moon, both a blessing and a curse. The night put him and Kirk at a distinct disadvantage, but they did have surprise on their side. Caywood listened and waited. When he saw the man approaching he held his breath, waiting until he had passed two steps beyond him. Quietly he stepped out behind Sare.

"Stop where you are, Sare."

The man whirled around and in one movement knocked Caywood down.

"Get him, Kirk. He's coming your way." Caywood was on his feet in a split second chasing after the man. He'd lost the torch and was running on pure instinct.

"He's heading toward the water," Copperfield shouted.

Kirk ran in that direction, stumbling on jagged rocks that were carpeted with snow, slick, slippery deception. There was a tremendous noise that echoed through the hills. Caywood stopped in his tracks. Snow plummeted from overhead branches.

"What's happened?"

"I've got him," Copperfield shouted. "Caught him," he struggled to say. "He's got a gun."

Caywood and Kirk, carrying torches, raced down to the river. When they reached an exhausted Copperfield, they relieved him of the burden of the gun and Sare. Struggling back up the hill, they got to the car safely.

Sare said nothing. Caywood told him of his wife weeping in Cheamley. There was no breaking the man's composure.

"Can I keep him in your station house until morning?" Caywood asked.

"Yes, of course."

"Well, let's go there and we'll leave for Rumsden after a few hours' rest. We can all use it, including Mr. Sare. That correct, Mr. Sare?"

The man said nothing.

CHAPTER 14

Confessor

At dawn the flight back to Rumsden was breathtaking. Caywood saw the waterfall and promised himself a holiday in the area. Tall green trees projected upward with snow decorating, outlining the sprawling branches. Sare remained silent. Caywood knew that every conceivable course of action was spinning through Sare's formidable brain. The man was secured to his seat with handcuffs. If he planned to escape it would be in Rumsden. Before they left, Caywood asked Copperfield to search the area for Sare's car—the man had to have had some means of transportation—and to check the registration as well. "Search the car and bring everything you find in to us. Mr. Sare," Caywood shouted over the roar of the engine, "we have Colin Clemson in custody."

Sare said nothing, but Caywood saw the information register and feed into the man's computer brain.

"Radio ahead for an extra hand and a secure van for the prisoner," Caywood ordered the police pilot. A tired Kirk nodded agreement. They settled down for the ride back.

The men went through the routine paperwork and, as quickly as possible, brought Sare to the interrogation room where Caywood and Kirk waited. None of them had had an easy night, and the fuses to their tempers were short.

"Sit down, Sare," Caywood ordered. "We have a fairly accurate history of your background and activities. We have two murders to tidy up, and believe me, I don't care at this point whom we select to be the guilty party. The three of you could be sent away forever."

Sare sat quietly, no emotion apparent. There was no increase in his rate of breathing, no sweating. He is, Caywood thought, the coolest character I've encountered.

"Let's have your version of this affair," Caywood said. "Who killed Quentin Stanley?"

"I'm sure I don't know, Inspector."

"Who murdered Hazel Weller?"

"I don't know that either," Sare said without a change of expression.

"Well, if that's the way it is to be, Mr. Sare, so let it be. I've sent for your wife. Perhaps she can help." Caywood waited for some sort of emotion, but there was no change in Sare's attitude. He signaled Kirk to lock the man up. "And then get Clemson back in here," Caywood ordered.

The man was still pale but considerably more composed than he had been the day before. Kirk sat behind him.

"Let's start where you left off, Clemson. Your friend is still downstairs ready to kill you, and now he has a helper. We have your other friend, Sare. When did Quentin start his blackmailing?" Caywood asked.

"Blackmail? Quentin never blackmailed anyone."

Caywood looked stunned. His best rug had been pulled from beneath his feet, and he was on his backside. "Then why was he murdered?" He could feel Kirk seething.

"We all shared equally, but Sare found out that when Quentin needed extra money he stole small pieces without replacing them. When Sare warned him that he would expose the setup, Quentin just laughed at him and went on as he pleased. We had a meeting and decided that we had to either quit or kill Quentin. We all had enough to live comfortably, but Quentin decided to make us all pay for the fact that he'd been duped, and he went on stealing regardless of what we said."

"Who killed Quentin Stanley?" Caywood asked.

"I don't know, Inspector, except that I didn't. We drew for it. Whoever got the black ball did it."

"You mean you drew straws for the job?"

"In a manner of speaking. The only one who knows is the one who did it."

"Put him downstairs, next to our friend the vicar."

"I'm telling you the truth, Inspector. Absolutely the truth. Please," he begged as he half rose from his chair.

"Downstairs cells, Kirk." Caywood got up to leave the office.

"All right, Inspector. I'll tell you the rest of it."

"Sit down, then, and get on with it."

"Eddie did it. We decided to stop Quentin before he got us all in trouble. We were satisfied with what we had and were ready to quit. Kevin—that is, Eddie—drew the mark. We steered Quentin to the church and Eddie met him in the woods behind the church. When he ran away toward the children he made Eddie very angry. He killed him on the spot."

"Did he leave him there? How did Quentin's body get to the graveyard?"

Clemson took a deep breath and said, "I did it. Eddie told me to wait until dusk and people were settled for the evening."

"But you didn't wait, did you?" Caywood asked.

"No, it began to snow and I thought I could get it done during the storm."

"What happened?"

"I heard children coming. I panicked and ran. I planned to come back later, but they found the body."

"And what about Hazel Weller?" Caywood asked.

"Eddie again. He went to tell her about Quentin. Told her that we would care for her the rest of her life if she kept quiet."

"But obviously she objected," Caywood said.

"Not at first, according to Eddie. She thought long and hard and decided that she didn't trust us to keep a promise."

"I wonder why," Caywood muttered.

"We could have, Inspector. It was to our advantage to do so, but she said Quentin had told her everything and that she wanted twenty thousand pounds immediately. She would either get that much and leave Cheamley or she would go to the police. She hadn't counted on Eddie's temper."

"That docile vicar?"

Clemson smiled sadly. "Yes, he killed her on the spot and planned to put her in the water. With the ice she would be there until spring."

"With no one to miss her? Surely you didn't think you could get away with that."

"Of course we could. We had the ladies of the church to believe whatever their good vicar told them. They would compound and embellish the story."

"Who helped him move the body?"

"I did. When I came out of The Angels, I saw Eddie and went to help."

"Why didn't you finish the job?"

"We hadn't counted on Tarlton making rounds as early as he did. We saw him coming and got out of the way. I went home and cleaned up and went to the pub."

"You realise that it's your word against Morgan's."

"Sare knows the truth and so does Mrs. Shaw."

"Mrs. Shaw?"

"Mrs. Shaw, Eddie's housekeeper, actually his wife. She knows the whole story."

"I'll check every word," Caywood promised. "Sergeant Kirk, put him in a cell on this level."

Sergeant Alcott passed Kirk as he took Clemson away. "Telephone for you, Inspector. It's Superintendent Rawleigh," Alcott said.

Caywood groaned audibly while Alcott smiled sympathetically.

"Yes, Superintendent." Caywood paused to listen. "Yes, sir. I believe we've broken the case now. Tying up loose ends now." Pause. "No, sir. I haven't seen the newspaper."

Caywood ran his fingers through his hair and frowned as he listened to his superintendent.

"I'll get a copy immediately, sir. Regardless as to what they say, we have the situation under control. It's a matter now of searching the village for the rest of the stolen goods and checking one more person."

Caywood maintained a scowl as he listened. "No, sir. I think I have enough men, but I appreciate your offer. Thank you." Caywood replaced the receiver and shouted for Alcott.

He came running and handed Caywood a newspaper. The headline said it all. TWELVE MUSEUMS REPORT THEFTS.

Caywood looked up and smiled at Alcott. "I think they missed a few. Get Sergeant Kirk for me. Tell him I want him to go to Cheamley."

CHAPTER 15

It's Over

Caywood brought her into his office, where Kirk was waiting with the vicar.

"Why is she here?" Morgan demanded angrily.

"Please sit down," Caywood said softly.

"She had nothing to do with any of this," Morgan insisted.

"Eddie, I'm all right. Please don't worry." She began to weep softly.

"Oh, Emily, I'm so sorry. Inspector, she had nothing to do with this. I did it all."

A spark of chivalry at long last in all of this, Caywood thought and leaned forward in his chair. He saw Eddie Morgan's facade beginning to crumble and waited, the silence in the office broken only with Mrs. Shaw's sobs.

"I killed Quentin, the mean old sod. He would have destroyed me and Emily without a second thought. We were all in this together, and we each did our share, but he had made up his mind to do as he wished without any regard for the consequences to us or to himself. He was a sorry wretch who believed he could do anything and get away with it. He threatened me and Emily and Collie and Des as well. He deserved to die." Morgan clenched his fists, anger destroying his usually smiling face. Even when he had been evasive in prior questioning, he had never looked as he did now. "Emily had nothing to do with any of this."

"She was aware that you were a fraud. She helped you maintain your position," Caywood said.

"No harm in that." Morgan was regaining his composure.

"The bishop might think otherwise, and we most certainly do."

"St. Mary's would have been closed. Those people would have had a visiting priest and nothing more."

"That's not in my province, so please, let's get back to the facts. How did you do it?"

"We decided one of us had to do it. We tossed for the honour, so to speak." Kevin Marsh, alias Edmund Morgan, smiled sadly. "I was glad, actually, for it to be me. We had decided I would have one last talk with him. He met me Wednesday in the woods behind St. Mary's. He came on time. I slipped out of the meeting. Not hard to do. I usually pop in and out of them. He met me, threatened me. There was no reasoning with him because he no longer cared whether he was caught or not, but then I realised he would destroy Emily as well, while he and that obnoxious Hazel Weller continued on. He started laughing and screaming obscenities at me and ran into the woods. The children were near. I heard Rose laughing. He called to them to go away, to run, to hide, as if I would harm a child. He ran after them into the woods, and when I caught him I forgot why I was supposed to kill him. I began beating him because he had made me so angry I couldn't abide the sight of him. I beat him with all the strength I had."

Emily Shaw dried her eyes and reached over to pat Kevin Marsh's hand. He buried his head in her lap and wept.

"Mr. Marsh, do try to pull yourself together. I have only a few more questions. Where is the weapon? I assume it was the same for both."

"Yes, Inspector, my heavy cane."

"Did you help him, Mrs. Shaw?"

Marsh answered, "She knew nothing about this until you came."

"And Miss Weller?" Caywood asked.

"She demanded money, several thousand pounds, or she would expose us all. She showed me some of the trinkets, as she called them, that Quentin had stolen for her. They would, of course, be missed. Quentin didn't bother to replace them with fakes. I couldn't stand the woman. She started laughing at me, said all the wise, rich men were going to dance to her tune and how she would enjoy it. I bashed her head in. How surprised she was. I finished the job so no one could recognise her and dragged her out in her wheelchair. When I got to the river, close to the edge, I stumbled and she fell forward. Collie knew I was to see her that night, so when I came up the bank, he was standing at The Angels and came to help me."

"You planned to put her under the ice?" Caywood asked.

"Yes, but P.C. Tarlton, the new man, was making his rounds. I heard his bicycle rolling onto the bridge, so we hid until he had passed and decided we would be missed. It looked like there would be a blizzard. We thought the snow would hide the body until we could complete the job."

"Where is all the silver and other things taken from Sare's in Harton?"

"In St. Mary's, I suppose."

"All of it? We've picked St. Mary's cleaner than a hound's tooth," Caywood said.

"You haven't looked in all the right places, Inspector. Sare always kept the best for himself. He always knew which was best."

"Then I shall take you and Mrs. Shaw back to Cheamley, where you can help us and have your house in order. You will, of course, have to return here, as will Mrs. Shaw."

"No, not Emily."

"Marsh, she was a party to the whole scheme. I have no choice. By the way, why have you kept your marriage secret?"

"We are married in God's eyes," Marsh said.

"God's?" Caywood murmured.

Caywood sent Kirk with the pair to Cheamley, and there, in St. Mary's, Kevin Marsh gave up a secret cache of small treasures that the police had missed. He returned the silver candelabrum from the altar and, when they returned to Rumsden, Emily Shaw took an ornate gold cross from about her neck and gave it to Harry Kirk.

The museums had presented the New Yard with a list of missing treasures. That list ultimately filtered down to Harry Kirk. Together with it and the inspector's book of lists the sergeant was totally overwhelmed. He rang up Miss Crisp, who agreed to help.

Caywood was taken aback by his sergeant's audacity and Eliza's anxious agreement.

"Be careful. She sounds too willing to me," Caywood warned.

"Good publicity for her store, close to Christmas and all that," Kirk persisted.

"She'll try to worm that Han thing away from you, Harry. I know her all too well. She'll find a way and then you'll be one sorry, sorry sergeant. I'll see to that. Now, get Mr. Sare back here."

Caywood made certain that Mrs. Sare had a private visit with her husband. She and the children would pay too great a price as it was. He remembered Sare's history and the price he'd already paid because of his parents' sorry life. Sergeant Alcott provided them a small room and placed a constable on guard outside the door.

"You didn't do any of this, Des, I know you didn't. You couldn't have." She dabbed her eyes with a small lace handkerchief and tried to smile.

"I haven't murdered anyone, darling, but you must be prepared to take care of the children by yourself for a while. Joe Ringel has instructions to provide money for you."

"How? How can that be?"

"Never mind the details. We haven't much time to talk. Just listen to me, please. Joe has enough silver and other things to sell once this affair has settled down. There will be enough money. Don't worry."

"But . . ."

"Listen to me. Go to your mother's. If need be, change your name if I am convicted. I think I can manage to get out of this. Joe will contact you. Contact Reach, my solicitor, as quickly as you can upon leaving here, then go to your mother's with the children." He stood up and held her close to him. "I love you very much. You're the best thing that has ever happened to me. Now, go and wait for me, please wait for me." He kissed her quickly and rapped on the door for the constable to take him away.

She stood there for a moment and wept, realising that he was deeply involved and that they might never be alone again.

Sare remained the same. He sat for an hour in Caywood's office and never answered a question. The arrival of his wife gave Caywood an opportunity to complete some paperwork. By the time he had finished, Eliza Crisp had come and gone without her Han cauldron.

"She was very angry, Inspector," Kirk said.

"I told you she would be, but I'm glad you stuck to your guns, Sergeant."

"Yes, sir. By the way, Mrs. Sare left, but Mrs. Clemson visited her son and is still waiting for a word with you."

"Bring her in right away, Harry. Poor soul."

She looked older than her years now. Her face covered by despair, Caywood helped her to a chair.

"Here, sit and rest a bit, Mrs. Clemson. What a sad time this is for you."

"I'm so disappointed in Colin," she said. "Where did I go wrong?"

"You are not responsible for what happened to a man during the war. Surely you know that."

"That retarded man is Colin's son. Did you know that, Inspector? His own son, pushed aside for someone else to care for. They thought it was a joke. I raised a totally amoral man. I can't believe it. I'll take care of James now." She let the words flood out in a torrent. "I'll go to St. Agnes and bring him back to live with me."

"You can't do that, Mrs. Clemson. The change would be too upsetting to him. You must let him stay where he is."

She began to sob, and Caywood put his arms around her shoulders and tried to comfort her.

Caywood drove her back to Cheamley and arranged for Miss Lydia Knight to stay with her. When he returned, Kirk told him that after Sare's visit with his wife he'd agreed to tell the whole story, provided the police would help him. Now they had it all tied up.

"There will be a promotion in this for you, Harry. Maybe that will help your home problem."

"I'm sure it would, Inspector. Maybe she'll listen to reason."

Eliza put the tray on the bedside table, leaned over, and kissed him. When he didn't awaken, she kissed him again. Caywood smiled and pulled her down beside him on his narrow bed.

"You've slept for twelve hours. I began to worry."

He held her close to him.

"I see you're in your usual form." She sat up. "There was no need to worry. Here's your tea. Ring me up when you're awake enough to make sense."

"I was making sense."

"Never mind, Peter. Call me later."

He jumped from the bed and fell on the floor when his left foot got tangled in the sheets. "Damn!"

She came back to find him spread-eagle on the floor. "Oh, for heaven's sake, Peter. Here." She threw his robe to him and sat on the bed while he put it on. "Have your tea and tell me about my cauldron."

He sat beside her and rubbed his left knee. "I knew there was a reason for all this solicitude. That bloody cauldron, is it?"

"Drink your tea, Peter." She smiled and handed it to him. "Now, where's my cauldron?"

"You're a witch."

"Yes, my darling." She kissed him.

"It's police evidence, Eliza."

"When do I get it back?"

He kissed her. "Soon, I hope."

"What does that mean?"

"After the trial."

"Oh my Lord. That may be years."

"Now, Eliza, you didn't miss it when it was stolen. Pretend it's at Regents, just where you and dear old Dad put it."

"It's not there. It's in the clumsy clutches of policemen. When you get it for me, Peter, ring me up." She slammed the door as she left the flat.

He smiled and knew she'd be back. But now that he was awake it was time to dress and get back to Cheamley and clean the rest of the business up. Maybe he'd see Caroline Clemson, but he hoped he wouldn't have to face her again. He was a coward about such things, and he knew it.

Two hours later he was in Cheamley. Caywood gathered up his briefcase and the boxes from the alcove in St. Mary's church hall. Now the ladies would be shed of them and have their domain back. He hoped they'd get a new vicar. He sat down and fetched a cigarette out of the black-and-silver case. A gust of cold air forced the gray smoke above his head. He still found it hard to believe, that this small band of greedy, hateful men had organised themselves into a force that undermined the world of fine art. The curators, the experts, the collectors all had been rooked by these conniving crooks. No one was certain as to what he had or what it was worth. What had started out as a joke among bored, disheartened men took shape, and they molded it into a business that was nurtured by the smug confidence of art's higher echelon. Caywood smiled when he thought about the public's reaction to the "haves." The common man was a bit more sympathetic to the crooks than to the duped. He tossed one cigarette stub into a tray and lit another. When he considered how these thieves destroyed themselves and had him totally fooled for much too long, Caywood shook his head in disgust. Then he smiled to think that the whole solution had been served to him by Eliza, in a cauldron.

He put out the last cigarette, gathered his boxes and case, and walked to the car. The snow was melting, the sun lit up Cheamley. Caywood passed over the north bridge for what he hoped was the last time. He thought he'd get some Chinese takeaway and go to Eliza's.

About the Author

Rosemonde Peltz is a physician. She lives in Decatur, Georgia. This is her first novel.